T0000794

IN EVERYTHING
I SEE YOUR HAND

STORIES

NAIRA KUZMICH

introduction by JOSIE SIBARA

UNIVERSITY OF NEW ORLEANS PRESS

In Everything I See Your Hand: Stories. Copyright © 2022 by Naira Kuzmich. All rights reserved. ISBN: 9781608012374.

Portions of this work have appeared in previous publications: "Anahit Number Eight" in *Puerto del Sol*, "Beginning Armenian" in *Arts & Letters*, "Eulogy for Rosa Garsevanian" in *Blackbird*, "In Everything I See Your Hand" in *Passages North*, "The Kingsley Drive Chorus" in *The O. Henry Prize Stories 2015* (originally appearing in *Salamander*), "Miles to Exit" in *West Branch*, "Transculturation, or: An Address To My American Lover" in *South Dakota Review*, and "Woman Amid Ruins" in *Ninth Letter*.

Cover and book design by Alex Dimeff. Cover illustration: "Punica granatum" by Pierre-Joseph Redouté from *Traité des arbres et arbustes que l'on cultive en France en pleine terre* by Henri-Louis Duhamel du Monceau, courtesy of rawpixel.com, available from: https://flic.kr/p/2eX652R.

Library of Congress Cataloging-in-Publication Data

Names: Kuzmich, Naira, author.
Title: In everything I see your hand : stories / Naira Kuzmich ; introduction by Josie Sibara.
Description: First edition. | New Orleans, Louisiana : University of New Orleans Press, [2022]
Identifiers: LCCN 2022005006 (print) | LCCN 2022005005 (ebook) | ISBN 9781608012374 (paperback) | ISBN 9781608012367 (ebook) | ISBN 9781608012367 q(ebook) | ISBN 9781608012374 q(paperback)
Subjects: LCSH: Armenian Americans--Fiction. | LCGFT: Short stories.
Classification: LCC PS3611.U975 I5 2022 (ebook) | LCC PS3611.U975 (print) | DDC 813/.6 23/eng/20220--dc01
LC record available at https://lccn.loc.gov/2022005006

First edition
Printed in the United States of America on acid-free paper.

UNIVERSITY OF NEW ORLEANS PRESS
2000 Lakeshore Drive
New Orleans, Louisiana 70148
unopress.org

advance praise for

IN EVERYTHING I SEE YOUR HAND

"If a god decided to write a book, what would it look and feel like? These stories by Naira Kuzmich provide a lens. Marked by a preternatural depth of feeling, and guided by a blinding intelligence, these stories evoke a modernist feel where the warp and woof of time and experience weave together a cosmos of simply and deeply soulful being. Here, in the world of these living souls, no moment goes untouched. Sorrow, Grief, Courage and Love— these are the recurring subjects in this astounding and wise, relentlessly honest and beautiful book. Enter the world and poetics of Naira Kuzmich, a talent like no other, and be amazed at the glory of being human. These stories: breathtaking."

—T. M. McNally, author of *The Goat Bridge* and *The Gateway*

"Her work cries out not just for Armenians, but for all tribes, all refugees, separated from homelands. 'Imagine here,' she wrote, 'the wail of the duduk.' Her gift of language has captured that sound on the page."

— Stuart Dybek, author of *The Coast of Chicago*

"She paid eloquent tribute to her mother, to her Armenian family and heritage again and again, in unforgettable stories. Thank god we have them. [...] She was in a hurry, fearless, eager for life and compelled to add her voice to it. Naira Kuzmich has left us a small but stellar body of work."

— Melissa Pritchard Schley, author of *A Solemn Pleasure*

"The grace of Naira's writing, the scale of her artistic vision, and the precision of her exquisite language illuminate her themes of cultural identity, displacement, and the experience of the Armenian Diaspora. [...] She is invested in the inherent musicality of language itself, especially as it may offer a lyrical voice to a silenced people. Simply, an extraordinary writer."

— Tara Ison, author of *Reeling Through Life: How I Learned To Live, Love & Die at the Movies*

CONTENTS

IN EVERYTHING I SEE HER HAND

I have no children of my own, but I imagine that upon giving birth a mother both recognizes her child as if they've always known each other and is shocked, too: the child is a mystery unfolding, belongs to herself as we all do. Naira was seventeen and in her first semester of college when she was randomly assigned to the rote and archaic composition course on topics in sociology for which I was, as I know now, lucky enough to be the teaching assistant. Naira revealed herself right away to be an exceptional student, the kind where you think: What am I going to *do* with her?

But it wasn't until the final assignment, in which students presented essays on a subject of their choice, that I truly understood what I'd been given. When Naira began reading her piece about her mother's hands, a revised few lines of which you'll find in this collection, my breath caught in my throat, and I could feel the others holding theirs as well, stunned: we had been all along in the presence of someone whose power to evoke character and mood, whose ability to use language, was on the level of *magic* or *miracle*, a thing you believe only if you encounter it yourself.

I told Naira she had a gift. Perhaps she should take a creative writing course second semester. She was skeptical, did not quite believe me. I recommended a few novels that might help her along the way, let her take them home with her. A few weeks later, we met at a coffee shop near campus, and she asked if I would teach her to write the kind of stories she wanted to write. Although I wanted nothing more, I said I wasn't qualified. I wrote mostly poetry; she should have an experienced teacher who could truly honor her talent.

When I was done, Naira raised her palm and held it to the side as she replied—a gesture I would come to know well over the years and which meant: *The rest of the world can believe what they will. But let us talk of what is real and cannot be compromised at the heart of this matter.* She wanted *me* as her teacher. I had not known that finding the one to whom you are supposed to impart your wisdom, however frail or inadequate it might be, had a feeling associated with it: such recognition, such shock.

So began a decade of trying to learn enough about writing prose to stay ahead of Naira's curve, no easy feat. Although she told me often how grateful she was, I don't think she ever grasped the depth of my own gratitude: I knew she was teaching me as much if not more about writing than I was teaching her. She was hungry for knowledge, came to my office and eventually, as we became friends, my home, with another question, another approach, another way to think about writing. Her stories grew more complex and nuanced, and she thought carefully about what she wanted to say and to whom. She was hard on herself, exacting, always believed she could have done better.

As I was preparing to write this, revisiting the territory in my heart reserved for my dear friend whom I can see no more, I dreamed I went with Naira's mother, Tagui, one of the loveliest human beings I've ever known, to Armenia so she could show me the places about which Naira wrote. When Tagui and I talked about this dream, she told me that even shortly before her death, Naira wished for just "a little more life," so she could travel to Armenia again, tell the world all she saw there; only then would she consider her mission done. Yet she had already written this book, which contains more stories than are listed in the contents: Naira was incredibly skilled at slipping whole and yet variegated histories between the lines, accomplishing more with her words and her approach than the surface suggests.

You might think it would be easy to teach a talented writer who possesses such focus and passion the mechanics of fiction, most of which I had learned a mere season before myself. And in some ways, that's true. Naira, intelligent as she was, gutted her way through these lessons. Her eye, however, was cast on something deeper that cannot be taught.

I cherish this memory: standing in my kitchen to enact a scene she'd written, demonstrating what was happening in the story's physical space that she'd left undescribed. A plate of Armenian pastries, each as beautiful and intricate as a wedding dress, sat on the table; Naira brought these each time she visited. She laughed at me moving my arms about, no doubt on a sugar high, and then said, dutifully, yes, maybe she'd left the reader a bit afloat—but then how had I figured out so exactly what Anahit was doing in the scene?

Meaning was what counted most of all. Carving out a backdrop that would reveal the depth of a character's plunge. Making beauty of this fleeting life's pain so that a reader felt they could—they must—go on despite the hurt. Where Naira could turn toward the devices of plot, she instead grasps at what I would call the ineffable but for her articulation of it. Each such moment a well-honed blade touching a stretched membrane that breaks fast away. Such as in "Anahit #8":

"What's it like?" I ask before I can stop myself.
"What's what like?"
"Disappearing?"

And a few moments later:

"Was the car there when we got here?" I ask her. "I don't remember how we parked if it was."
The Corvette suddenly lurches forward, like it might have been waiting for us to notice it before it drove off. We watch it go until it disappears into the horizon, past the main intersection.

We've been trained by fiction's conventions to expect the Corvette to cause some shenanigan, but instead, we see how very much life is for these characters about noticing—being seen—and disappearing. Standing before the chasm revealed by the first bit of dialogue, you find yourself somehow mourning a car simply driving away, reminding us of the horizons that only seem to separate us.

Naira's vision regarding human connection belied her age. She wrote about truths that seemed to come from a dream I had already had, long ago, one that had affected my whole life's path. These feelings weren't limited to me, lest you think me perhaps just an overweening teacher. Another Armenian friend, a man forty years Naira's senior, spoke of how her stories embodied Armenia, yes, but how it went beyond that, as if she had read something in his soul.

And indeed what Naira's characters most often attempt to do is read the souls of others, to "learn things about them they don't want me to know, that they don't know themselves, or think they don't. The last part's the hardest to figure out, because no one ever thinks they're just pretending." Naira knew more than a person can in one lifetime, which doesn't for one moment make up for how little life she got. And she did not let people pretend—not in fiction, not in life. In everything I see *her* hand guiding me toward words like "soul" and "truth," leading me to believe that even if I wanted to hide, she would have known me anyway. You may, in these pages, find that she knows you too.

This introduction can never do justice to Naira the writer. You hold her dream in your hands and can find your own proof in these pages: she was brilliant and what she had to say was important and world-changing. It has indeed been one of my life's greatest privileges to witness her growth as an artist. And I feel yet another chasm opened out into the years ahead that her beautiful words would have filled. I play her stories back, hoping they'll echo there. Once you've read her words, I am certain they will be your balm as well, that you will become one of the people keeping Naira the writer alive.

Although she's never far from my mind, it is harder sometimes for me to speak of Naira the person, yet I must: Naira's lesson demands it of me. For creative people, especially those who use the material of their lives in their work, the two are intertwined, so we sometimes forget that there is a self who hovers before the blank page, and she can never be written down. You know her only in flesh and blood and long hours spent talking, by how her hair flies in the wind when she's standing on a cliff overlooking the sea in Ireland with the man she loves and is truly happy. Watching her devour a piece of cake as if it is the last on Earth. Her sense of hilarity. Her compassion.

The blade to my heart is losing Naira, herself. Her thoughts, her dreams, the part of her that existed even outside the bounds of what we can know even about a fiercely loved other, a concept that brings me great comfort now, as perhaps that part of a person we can never know persists most easily beyond death. *Fiercely*, she would say at the end of each of her letters. *I love you fiercely*. It was one of the last things she ever said to me. Had Naira taken up long-distance truck driving or lawyering halfway through the years we were given, I would have yet loved her as my friend, my sister, my child, one of my witnesses in this life.

Because she *was* my witness and her love was fierce, Naira made me want to become a person worthy of being in her presence. She understood how to love better than I did; she was *my* teacher yet again in this regard. But this is not the after-the-fact realization of a grieving friend: Naira made sure everyone knew how important they were to her, how much each moment meant.

One night my partner and I were having dinner with Naira and her fiancé Vedran in Chicago, and it started to snow. Naira, having grown up in Los Angeles, hadn't seen much snow, although she had written of it in stories taking place in Armenia. She said, *Let's go!* So the two of us left the restaurant and stood beneath a streetlamp and watched it swirling in that gold glow that also lit up her young face. She turned and embraced me then so sudden and tight I felt the shock, recognition: we were supposed to know each other. *Thank you*, she said. *For everything. This is so beautiful.*

When I read our correspondence from years ago or her final weeks, it strikes me that we were always having the conversations some have only when they know they will lose each other. Imagine that your words spoken to friends at the end of your life are only a reiteration of the love you have given generously throughout. Naira did this without even knowing it was incredible. And those of us who knew her, whether in person or through her writing, will spend the rest of our lives saying to her: *Thank you. For everything. It was so beautiful.*

—*Josie Sibara*

JOSIE SIBARA is the author of *The Galaxie and Other Rides*, a collection of stories about growing up in post-industrial Detroit. Her book of poems, *living must bury*, was published by Fence Books. She is a graduate of the University of Southern California's dual Ph.D. Program in Literature and Creative Writing; her doctoral dissertation focused on literature and climate change. She has been a resident at The Sitka Center for Art and Ecology, The Millay Colony, The Studios of Key West, and Willapa Bay AIR. Josie also completed a PEN Northwest Wilderness Residency, during which she lived for six months on a remote homestead above Rogue River in southern Oregon's Klamath Mountains. She received a National Endowment for the Arts Literature Fellowship. The draft of her first novel won the James Jones First Novel Fellowship. A work of long fiction, "The Man on the Beach," was published as a Ploughshares Solo. Josie recently completed a novel and is at work on another.

IN EVERYTHING
I SEE YOUR HAND

BEGINNING ARMENIAN

With 38 letters, the Armenian alphabet is one of the richest in the world.

Every day I stand in front of a classroom full of women who resemble my mother and teach them things they already know but pretend they don't. They just want an easy A, credits to get their Associate's Degree, a certificate they don't yet know won't be of any use to them by the time they graduate. If they graduate. Most of them won't. Most will drop out in a semester, having collected their federal funding and forgotten to reapply for aid for the following year. It's not bad money: usually two, three thousand every four months, money that goes towards rent, towards buying name-brand shoes for their sons, supporting relatives back home.

It's a classroom of actresses with leftover Soviet accents. They bring me fresh *byoreks* from their ovens, invite me to their homes for a cup of *surj*. They say, Professor Chopuryan, you are Armenian woman, you know what we have to do at home, so much work. They say, But Professor Chopuryan, we stay up all night after children sleep, husband has eaten, house is clean, mother-in-law is happy, and do a lot of homework for you.

But it's not a lot of homework. Maybe it is for the two white Americans and one Filipino in the class, but it's certainly not a lot for them. Just two or three pages of exercises from children's books that they already owned before stepping foot in my classroom, books that they force their young ones to read, maybe on the weekend, an hour or two hunched over the dining room table.

I can picture it so clearly: the little feet tapping against the carpeted floor, the longing glances behind the shoulder and through the window, the whining, the pleas, the please, please, pleases. And the women with their floral house-dresses, their generous breasts, stirring pots or folding grape leaves around steaming rice, rolling their eyes and raising their hands in threat. You will not leave this table until you have finished that page.

We have all been raised like this, spoon-fed our language as if it were an unsavory bowl of meat-soup. I had to wait until I was eighteen before I could leave my mother's table without her permission.

There is a great respect for the object of a sentence, as it always comes before the verb.

My mother never hit me after we came to America. Lord knows she wanted to, and Lord knows how often she prayed to Him to forgive her for the thought, but if my mother was good at one thing, it was learning how to adapt to new environments. In Los Angeles, you could kill a man and get away with it, but you could not touch your children.

"Not even a little smack?" she asked our neighbor, Mariam, after we moved into the dinky old apartment on the corner of De Longpre and Kingsley. I was seven, she thirty-two. Our neighbor was not amused.

"It's not like it is back home. Be careful. Don't raise your voice too loudly at her in stores. Americans love getting involved. Tell your husband not to hug her too often or too fiercely. The things people think here."

I realized then that it was I who was in charge here, not my mother. If I wanted to, I told her one time after a fight, I could call the cops on her and allege verbal abuse.

"You know what that means, Ma? Verbal abuse? Do you?"

I had also made another discovery by then, that I already knew more words in English than she. "Virginity," she asked me one night after hearing the term on a talk-show. "What is this?" When I answered, she asked me how I knew. And because I didn't know what to tell her, I said nothing, and she pushed me back onto my bed and checked.

Question marks don't come at the end of sentences, only over certain words, certain vowels, always in the beginning.

At nineteen, I drove my mother to the doctor's office and took the test so she wouldn't have to do it alone.

"Jackie's mother was diagnosed last year," I told her during my spring break back home from college. "And she's a teacher."

My mother laughed. "What does that have to do with anything?" Jackie was my friend since elementary school, since we found out we were the only two Armenian girls in our 4th grade class and that both of our mothers were teachers. Jackie's mom was a substitute and mine had taught kindergarten back in Leninakan for a few years, but these were minor differences. It was pretty clear to us we were the same person. "It could've been you," I said.

So we went.

Her breasts were placed on a firm flat panel and then compressed gently with another.

"Mom, this is what they call a mammogram," I said, crossing the room to sit by the door. I had been standing behind her, and she seemed so old to me with her back naked, her high-waisted jeans pushing at the skin. I had wanted to see her face.

"The discomfort will last only a few seconds," the doctor said before he turned to me. "Then, it will be your turn."

I thought there had been a mix-up when he put the X-rays up on the board. It wouldn't be the first time someone confused me for my mother. I had her eyes, her upturned nose. Everyone said the two of us could be sisters. Mom looked her age. I didn't. My body developed early, caught men's attention too soon.

"But I'm still a kid," I said when the doctor gave us the news. "Mom?"

And my mother answered. She unbuttoned her blouse with the skill of an eager lover, something I had never known. She pulled the blouse off her pale, bright skin and threw it to the floor. As she fumbled to unclasp her bra, the doctor raised his hands in protest.

"Madam, madam, what are you doing?"

She dropped her bra to the ground and stepped over it to reach him. I watched as she grabbed her bare breasts and presented them to the doctor, like a gift, an exchange.

"It is me," she said. "I am the one. It is me who you want."

Most words cannot change into the feminine; whole new words must be invented for them.

I had yet to sleep with a man. I was nineteen, and the only person my breasts had brought down to their knees was my mother. I took a poetry workshop when I returned to school. I wrote things like "Sadness is for immigrants and this is America" that classmates called sentimental. In college, I had already learned how to speak eloquently about Communism, Feminism, Nihilism, subjects with capital letters. Capitalism. I was good at saying things I didn't mean or understand, then or since. Thanks to my lessons with my mother, I had a mind for memorization. I could spout back blocks of text from dull books or proverbs that the skinny boys and hungry girls in my mother's books tried to teach me. But finding my voice, making this language my own, was harder. I thought the poetry class would help. And I thought, too, that it would cure me. Art for the soul, as well as for the body, and all that.

There was a chance that the chemo would make me infertile, and somehow this knowledge was scarier than the chemo itself. I slept with five men in the course of four months in an effort, I later realized, to get pregnant. I used to hate children, but to be robbed of the decision to not have them, to not have a choice in the matter, what could be worse to a blossoming feminist? The sex was terrible, every part, the games that led to it, the act itself. I never came.

The guys were from class, all five, two of them good friends. One may have written about it the following week, I'm not sure.

I found out that, as with sex, I wasn't very good in poetry. People took too much time saying what they wanted to say—I am miserable, my life sucks, my lover was a frigid bitch, etc. But, Sona, everyone tried to explain to me: it's not what you say, but how you say it. This meant write it in the most ambiguous language possible. Or "let people decide for themselves what you are saying." This meant when talking to a potential employer on the phone, disguise your accent. Or "your mother will never belong in this country." This meant breast cancer is rare for someone your age, but not uncommon. Or "I'm sorry you are dying, but you are not the only one."

A double negative does not make a positive in Armenian.

My mother married my dad because she didn't have a reason not to. He was good-looking, he had a job, owned a car—a white LADA that he parked in her front yard the day he proposed, leaving the door open as if to say, this won't take long. He had heard there was a beautiful woman in the outskirts of Leninakan, black hair, big eyes, big hips. He knocked on the door to see for himself, and her father let him in. My mother was in the kitchen. When her father finally called her out and asked her to take a seat, she didn't pick the empty one next to her suitor. She reached for a dining room chair and sat down beside her father. This is, my dad tells me, when he knew that she was the perfect woman for him. It's his favorite story now that she's dead.

Growing up, my dad had one dream: that I'd find a man so captivated by me that he'd live in the same house as his in-laws. My dad was a man of numbers. Because he had only a daughter and wife then, his numbers didn't add up to what he had always wanted: a total of people who would worship the ground he walked on and eventually the one he'd be buried in. My dad wanted to be remembered more than anything. He wanted mourners, visitors to his grave, a lot of writing on his headstone. He wanted people to toast to his life long after it was over. He hoped his friends would laugh and cry as they took swigs from a bottle of his favorite whiskey, wanted his family to weep at every familiar scent. Like me, he was an only child, but he was one by accident. His brother died as a young man, smart and strong by all accounts, perfect at sixteen, when my dad was only eight. His parents never recovered, and so he spent the rest of his life trying to make them happy, trying to make them forget, but the son they forgot was the son they still had. All of my father's birthdays were quiet.

I say this not to defend him, as my mother often accused, but to provide context. Stories without context are only words, meaningless, that which can never amount to something greater than their root. In that sad medical office, all those years ago, I stole from my mother her happy ending and from my father his life-long dream.

My mother spent the last five years of her life battling early-onset dementia.

Adjectives are steadfast; while the noun it's describing may change in number, the adjective remains the same.

Illness in a family can either break or strengthen it, and there was never a time when I thought we'd fall apart. My parents were, in their own ways, people of action. I kept them busy. Dad put in more hours to pay my bills, my mother worried. The summer I came home from school, after my failed dalliances in poetry and sex, I began my treatment.

Young women with breast cancer are treated aggressively. Doctors try to leave no chance for the human spirit to weaken, for it to play a part. They think that young patients aren't as resilient, that they generally have not been tested. He recommended that I have my left breast removed. A mastectomy. The tumor clocked in at 1.96 centimeters, small enough to have a lumpectomy, a procedure that could've saved most of my breast tissue, but he didn't want to risk it. Do you want to risk it, he asked. And what could I tell him—that a man had yet to touch that left breast with love, yet to stand quiet, in awe, of my body, at the foot of my bed?

Of course not, I told him. Get rid of the whole thing.

Before the surgery, I told my father to buy a lot of plastic chairs, just in case, for all the mourners. Our apartment was too small and they'd have to remember me outside in the backyard, where I had first jumped rope without a bra. Months later, drunk and in the dark, I'd jump again, staring at the expanse where my left breast used to be, my vision blurring until I saw what I wanted. My mother watched me from the living room window.

The surgery went as planned and as hoped. After a course of chemo, we can talk about reconstructive surgery, the doctor said. So I did that too, lost my hair at twenty, bought my first wig, then my second, wore chest expanders, got the implant. I was back in school two years later, finished with my treatment at twenty-two, college at twenty-four.

Looking back, I don't want to say it was easy, but that it was merely easier than my mother thought it would be. It was easier than my mother's long dying.

All that energy in our bodies, those magical neurons, the little synapses and nerves that shine and sparkle in recognition and memory, all of that is for the young, but for what? There wasn't much I needed to remember.

Adjectives derived from proper nouns are not capitalized.

Disease is a language my mother never could master.

My official diagnosis was *secretory carcinoma*, and when I first heard it, I thought it sounded sexy, something quiet and foreign slithering out of the doctor's lips like a promise: don't even worry about it, kid. My mother didn't have the same reaction. To her, the more syllables a word had, the worse the prognosis. She couldn't hold all of breast cancer's strange vocabulary inside her mouth, so words like metastasis, alopecia, adjuvant therapy were butchered relentlessly. She'd spit them out, one after another, losing vowels, biting the heads off consonants. These words only meant one thing, that her daughter was sick, and this was something she couldn't cure with her home remedies. I remember eating teaspoons of granulated dark coffee to stop diarrhea or dipping lemon wedges inside the sugar bowl and sucking greedily to rid my sore throat. For headaches, I wore potato skins on my forehead; for sunburns, I bathed in tomato juice. When treatment started, these once minor ailments took on new and dangerous forms, and my mother put away her vegetables, her spices and powders, and saved the doctor's number onto her phone, taped the directions to the four closest pharmacies to her dashboard.

She was full of questions during the two-and-a-half years I underwent treatment. What does this mean? What do we do next? Couldn't you write a nicer poem?

Though I wasn't any good, I couldn't stop writing. I was eager to return to school and try workshop again. I had a feeling my sentimentality would be a lot more tolerable once my classmates learned that my left breast was a fake.

I made the mistake one time of letting my mother read. After an early session of chemo, she walked into my bedroom with another question: do you want to talk? I was tired, I really didn't want to, but I never wanted to. This time, though, I was too tired to say no. She sat by my side and patted down the sheets, saw my notebook on the nightstand and began flipping through it. She read one aloud, a silly poem about nothing, about anger, about being young and beautiful and diseased. She hesitated over the curse words, and there were a lot of them. Sona, she asked softly. Why must you use these bad words? People will think you are loose. There must be another way to say what you are feeling.

And I laughed, laughed as deeply as I could. Like that, I said. Is that any better?

The indefinite article always follows the noun to which it belongs.

I taught ESL after college. Spent a year in Korea, another in Romania. The job was unrewarding, but I had a fondness for travel and needed a good enough reason. My parents began having trouble around that time, fighting over the littlest of things now that I was out of the picture and in remission. Empty-nest syndrome, I would tell her from across the seas. Yes, her crackly voice would come through the receiver. Your father, the pigeon.

After my stints abroad, I returned to Los Angeles, found a job as a copywriter and an apartment far from my parents' home. They had thought I'd move back in with them and were disappointed when I didn't. I wasn't even dating. My father, concerned, tried to set me up with one of his old-man coworkers. But my mother, she was devastated.

"What will we do when we are old, Sona *jan*? Who will bring us a glass of water?"

I told them they weren't the first people to age in this country. There were resources.

"And where is our Sona?"

I'd help when I could, I said. But Sona was trying to live her own life.

Four years later, tired of my job and with no prospects for a promotion, I looked into graduate school. Change was good when you sought it, not when it found you, so I applied to several programs and ended up in Berkeley, doing a Ph.D. in Ethnic Studies. I was interested in ethnicity like all immigrants are interested in ethnicity, to validate our silly and difficult lives, but I was no expert and had no desire to be one. I just wanted new friends, a new city to walk, some distance. By this time, my parents had begun to talk to me one-on-one, more and more often. I'd get calls from my mother, complaining about how much he spent on bulk-sized alcohol or how loud he spoke on the phone with his friends, how frequently they came over. He'd tell me about her coldness, how she went weeks without washing her hair, how she grumbled about making breakfast on the weekends, forgot to put salt on his eggs.

When I was living in LA, I answered all these calls in person, sitting in their living room and nodding profusely. My mother would be in the kitchen, or in the bedroom, my father on the balcony, smoking. Despite their troubles, they were always sure to give each other space, give each other alone time with me. When

I was around, they were courteous and kind, saying each other's name before each request: Armineh, the phone, please; Garnik, the volume on the TV.

But I was no mediator, only their child. They were getting older, but they weren't the only ones. I was thirty, living in a studio apartment, working a dead-end job, no boyfriend. I had many reasons to pack my bags, so I did.

The possessor must in Armenian precede the object possessed.

I finished my doctoral studies with a diploma, and I suppose that was enough. I started teaching in San Francisco. Professor Sona Chopuryan, it had a good ring to it, like it was meant to be. That's what my mother said when I visited them in the summer after my first year teaching. You have gone far, my girl, she said, to be somebody. This isn't as ambiguous or meaningful in Armenian—my mother meant I had gone far literally, as in distance. She never spoke in symbols, in metaphors. She said what she saw, and what she saw was black and white: my daughter here, my daughter there, Armenia, America.

One afternoon, back home and sleeping on my parents' couch, my mother asked if I'd like a cup of coffee with her. My father was at work, though he was pushing sixty-five then, working the furnaces at a local jewelry business. We had just had lunch. I wasn't much of a coffee drinker, hating the tar taste of our Armenian *surj*, but sometimes I convinced myself I liked the bitterness on my tongue. My mother went to the kitchen, and I sat in the living room, flipping through a journal. I read one story about a celebrity scandal, then another. When my mother returned, she was holding a glass of water. She placed it in front of me on the table, and I laughed, said, Changed your mind, Ma? She smiled a small smile, sincere but hesitant. About what, she asked. I raised my eyebrows. The coffee, Ma. Would you like a cup, she said happily, standing up.

I thought she was just getting older.

The second person singular is used only among the common people.

It's not easy to take care of someone who doesn't know why she needs to be taken care of. At first, I only came home a weekend a month, sitting with my mother and telling her about my students, my new friends, describing the paintings I purchased in extraordinary detail. I called more often than I used to. I gave my father addresses for respectable homes that would take both of them in. He refused, as did my mother, in the beginning, when she still had choices, could still make them. She was only sixty when diagnosed. One time she left the house and came back seven hours later from God knows where. She certainly didn't. I began coming home twice a month. My tickets were round-trips. I'd brush her graying hair—though she still had plenty of black—and I'd tell her about my cat, Lola, the time she vomited in my shoes, my favorite restaurant on Mission Street, the bum on the bus beside me who hollered, "You think your shit doesn't smell like shit?" when I asked him to stop touching my leg. Another time, my mother knocked over a vase and walked over the glass, feet bleeding, to get to the ringing phone. It was me on the other end. More than once she attacked my father with whatever she could get her hands on—a pen, a spatula, tweezers—thinking him a stranger. I started coming home every weekend.

And it's not like it is in the movies. There are no happy endings, because there's no real story, because you forget to ask for one. Because you forget, too, sitting there in front of your disappearing mother, that you're not talking just to fill the silence. You forget that you should be listening, trying to piece together everything she says, every delusion and nonsense memory. Every strange thing, you should've written down, you should've recorded every scary laugh. You should've tried to keep her talking even as she started crying when she lost her train of thought. You should've asked more questions. You should've known how she'd answer. But sitting there in front of your disappearing mother, you were thinking this is the hardest thing I have ever done and you were thinking, dear God, haven't I been through enough?

The only one who believed in you was your mother. The doctor was right to take your breast.

Armenian is the only surviving link to the dead languages of Summerian, Hattic and Urartian.

After her funeral, in my black dress, I drove to the airport and booked the first flight to Yerevan. I aged in sixteen hours. I set foot in our country wearing her old shoes, a little tight around the ankle. I took a taxi to the city center, and the driver didn't recognize me. He didn't talk, I did. I talked and talked, saying nothing. I paid a *cigani* woman to tell me about the city when it was beautiful. She laughed while the baby at her breast cried. Pay me as much as you want, girl, but I can't remember that far back.

I had two addresses on a yellow Post-It. I had Google map walking directions in my hands. I stopped strangers and asked them, Do you know where I'm going? Crossing the wide streets was impossible; no one paid attention to the red lights. On the sidewalk, a grandfather held onto my elbow and we walked fast. On the other side, he pushed me towards a gang of women who tried to make me buy the wool stockings they were selling. I kept walking until I stood in front of my parents' home, my old house. No one lived there anymore. I peered through the bushes of the backyard for clues. Overgrown weeds, a wire fence.

I tried my luck somewhere else. I took a *mashutni* to Leninakan. Imagine a minibus but the height of a car. A young man with a sad mustache stooped the entire ride. I wanted to rip it off his face. I got out and walked the streets of my mother's youth. I wondered if there were any boys, any men here who had loved her, who loved her still, wrote her poems. I passed by more elderly women, their hair covered, all their skin covered, apron-ed. They didn't look at me the way I looked at them. I heard them complain about their daughters-in-law, I heard them praise their beauty. I kept walking. I took the long way. I hoped someone would stop me and say, You look familiar. I thought I arrived where I was supposed to be, where my mother was for so many years, but I may have been mistaken. There were people inside, I heard them. The front yard was not well kept, but it was well used. There were buckets for the apricots. I thought I could hear singing. I walked back, breathing hard. There was a kid on a dirty bike driving slowly in spirals beside me, staring at me a little funny when I turned to look. I dug through my purse and found two pens, a pack of gum. Here, I said, thrusting it at him. Go away, *gna, gna.* He took them from my hand and got off the bike, watched until I was gone, out of his view, out of his country.

The colon is not a colon, but a period. It is two fistfuls of dirt, one on top of the other. It is not a permission to speak or to sing.

If there is a God, then we deserve to be in sorrow only three times in our lives: at birth, at the weddings of our children, and then the minute before our passing. While I was undergoing treatment, my mother was trying to make deals with the devil. Ten years off mine for every extra year you give her. A wrinkle around my eyes for every month you keep her alive. My breast for her breast. Mind for her body.

My mother died a million deaths.

I want to say that I died right there along with her, but that would be a lie. *Soot* as we say in Armenian, like dirt, absolute shit. I'm back in LA, alive and well. I'm standing in front of a class-room, teaching middle-aged women how to read and write in a language they already know. My students claim to be from the village, all twenty-eight of them. Yes, Professor Chopuryan, we speak Armenian, but Mother and Father never taught us how to spell our names or read letters. Cows to milk, floors to wash, wet clothes to hang, lots to do, and so forth and so much. And I want to believe them, every single one. Nazik Chatinyan with her out-landish highlights and purple eyebrows, imitation Gucci blouses. Anahit Hagopyan, beautiful and quiet, graying hair and a purse full of tissues and pictures. Gayane Poghosyan, mother of four, chipped nails and cheap mascara. Perhaps they are all from the village, maybe not the same one, but did I not pass many while in Armenia?

So I listen to these women's stories and nod in the right places. I smile and sympathize and take them for their word. I look at their faces and tell them, Go on, I'm listening.

Tell me everything. *Soots* or truths.

Talk. Say anything, anything at all.

WOMAN AMID RUINS

"Spitak was the one town that was thoroughly destroyed.
Nothing survived. Nothing."
—Vona Gasparian
Head of Spitak's Department of Construction & Architecture

They found little Zara like this: standing below the mandarin tree, licking her palm. She was a shade between ashen and brown, except for her fingers, polished white with her tongue. When she tells her husband the story on their wedding night, she explains that the first lick was simply an instinct to clean. In her mouth, the residue of fresh snow, fruit, and reinforced cement. Her mother would be mad. No sweets before lunch, and certainly no going out after she had just showered. Her hair was wet, but when they found her, the townspeople felt Zara's head for a different kind of dampness. The mandarins she loved, but the snow even more, weighing down the tree's branches so she could grab at the fruit without jumping. She always hated exercise, Zara tells her husband, turning her head back to wink.

In the darkness of their bedroom, the darkness that comes before lovemaking, Zara sits at the edge of the mattress and rolls down her pantyhose. This is her favorite part of the day, shedding the second skin to let what's underneath expand. The hairs on her upper thigh stiffen, and she rubs them down slowly, in long strokes, like she is flattening dough, reaching the knees and pulling the flesh.

Zara, her new husband calls out in a playful whisper. Za-ra.

It was after eleven, she continues. Her brother was in school, and then was not, like all those children were not. She was ghost-like under the tree, but the townspeople who found her compared her to something else. A man raised her in the air, then put her down, almost pushed her away, and then he ran. And then, another man. And then, another. Not like a trophy, but a figure of luck. Perhaps, perhaps. Good fortune. Perhaps. They ran, looking for other children. But it was just she. In this neighborhood, in this part of Spitak, that great white city, this close to the primary school, it was just she.

Zara's husband sits up, spreads his legs around her legs, and wraps his arms around her waist from behind. She doesn't shy away from his touch, like he expects from his lovely bride, but she's still talking, she hasn't stopped, and, really, is this not the same thing?

So how does a village treat their only child after an earthquake, Zara asks her husband as he begins to kiss her neck. Or the Danes, the French, the Italians who come in terrifying machines from the sky over the next two weeks? There were candies, of course, and dolls with buttons for eyes that she had to turn around in order to hug. Zara remembers smelling the fabric of distant places, her nose nestled between manufactured American cotton. And there were tears, plenty of that, too. Embraces that went on too long, some which hurt her ribs, or hands that held her firmly by the biceps to tell her what a lucky little girl she was, fingers that bruised. Did she ask for her mother? Every day.

Do you know what your fingers taste like when you're a child? Like nothing special, but something entirely yours. A comfort in that, to feel in your mouth just you, your mouth occupied by just that, you and maybe the air you're breathing, but that's it. But then you're licking, and you're clean, and suddenly you don't recognize what you're tasting. What is that bitterness? What is that strangeness in your mouth?

Lie down, Zara tells her husband, and when he does, he takes her with him. She raises her head from the pillow, almost in question, and when he inches forward, this: They took me to the orphanage in Kirovakan, and the women there thought I was sick. Post traumatic something. I was licking everything. The wooden table all the motherless children shared for dinner and coloring. Licked the other children, too, and the women's headscarves— those, I remember, tasted like photographs, slick and grainy, or what photographs should taste like, but the photographs they had salvaged for us from the rubble tasted different: My brother sitting at the table, only his ears visible behind the wine bottle, and my father standing beside him, his hand disappearing behind the bottle to rest on his shoulder as he toasts to our future— that didn't taste like New Year's Eve, but like glass, cold, sharp, and, in parts, sticky. Or my mother in her red dress, dancing in our living room, eyes closed and clutching at the hem, revealing porcelain thigh. That, I remember, tasted like raspberry seeds, the remnant of the fresh burst still coating that hard shell.

And what do you taste like, husband, Zara asks. Standing now, he pushes her back gently, leans over her, hovers so he does not seem eager—this being his second wife. Zara takes his hand and places it on the area between her breasts, presses her hand over his, presses down. Here, bone, sternum. Their bed is a king, with two nightstands serving as posts, small soldiers of the evening scramble. A wallet is on his side, a glass of water on hers. Their closet is a walk-in behind a mirror, but she didn't have much when she came to Los Angeles a week ago, and so it still smells of her new husband's deodorant spray. She had closed the mirror-door, but the smell keeps seeping between carpet and glass, and the smell is so distinctly his that Zara can't pretend she is somewhere else, with someone she loves more.

She wiggles from under him and stands in front of the closet, the mirror.

Zara, he whispers again, and she thinks her name is like an incantation, how often he says it, with such feeling. But an incantation to what? What can she make happen, what can she give him that someone already hasn't taken?

She lifts her expensive nightgown over her head, setting it down beside him, the straps right below the pillow, the hem beside his knees. Her mother-in-law's present to Zara, aside, of course, from her son. *You're beautiful*, he tells her, and his voice comes from deep within him, as if across oceans, rumbling. *Your legs, dear God.* She stares down at the nightgown and smiles, trails her fingers across the satin. *There's something about the first touch. You think nothing has ever felt this good, this clean, that here lies the answer to everything.* She lies down on the nightgown because that is the only way to wear it. *The fabric that once fit you obscured by your back, the expanse of your skin glowing from the window's reflection of the moon. You, girl, who thought you would be here now?*

She reaches for her glass without looking, raises herself on one elbow to drink. Sets it down, keeps talking. *When they began building the SOS Kinderdorf, I was taken to Kotayk along with my orphanage friends, Armineh and Hovsep, who in their own ways too were special, who survived when their houses crumbled in Kirovakan and in Stepanavan. We had a new mother, Gertha, and seven new brothers and sisters. I was already forgetting Gokor, and though I kept a photo of my brother in my socks—Gokor tall and long-legged, big lips at eight, grinning eyes-closed into the camera, on the couch in just his underwear, bowl of sunflower seeds in front of him—he was tasting different, less and less distinct. And my mother, you ask? And my father? My mouth would dry, spit gone and not coming back, and I'd stare into my brother's lap, at that bowl of dried black tears, and I felt the shards between my teeth, and they tasted like nothing.*

I know, husband, you too have been hurt. Zara tugs at the small chunks of hair that decorate the scar on his chin, keep it hidden from view. She puts her leg around his hip, straightens, straddling him. Her breasts on his chest, she parts the hairs away with nimble fingers until the scar is visible. *Not all women are like this*, she tells him, moving her ring finger across the wound. The diamond on her finger doesn't catch the light from the window because it is not a diamond. It does not taste like Gertha's earrings or the ring Hovsep showed Armineh before she cried and turned away, turned him down, when they were all fifteen and fake siblings, fake people, ghosts. And down Hovsep went, too, down, down, until he too was buried.

The scar reaches from his chin down to his neck, and he was lucky, Zara tells her husband, that his first wife didn't cut deeper. Gertha would make us sing before dinner, she continues, our hands holding each other. At first I thought it was a punishment, but then grew to miss it at all the hours I was not touching someone and singing. It felt just like licking, like something about to fill your insides, but only about to. Satisfaction in the possibility. Pleasure in the hope. Picture ten boys and girls around a wooden table—it was hard, strong, tasted like apples—swaying, singing, faces eager to please dear Gertha, Gertha clapping to keep us on beat, busy hands used for more important things than laying the table where her Armenian children sat hungry and singing.

She did not hurt me, Zara laughs, when her husband grabs her pillow, puts it behind his head, and asks, though she sees he is mostly staring at her breasts. I cannot be hurt. She kisses his cheeks when she sees them blush. They taste like undershirts, washed by hand, still smelling like cheap soap. My wife was unfaithful, he says, voice sharp and sudden, like the breeze that shook the mandarins, And still I am the one to blame? I who must wear the burden on my face?

Armineh and I moved to Yerevan when we were sixteen, Zara says in response. She was leaving behind Hovsep, who had asked for her hand and then disappeared into himself when she had said no, brother, no, and I, tired of Gertha's songs and the sound that sprang from my own belly at the dinner table, went with her. Zara smiles at her husband and kisses his scar, then turns toward the window, thinking.

Zara and Armineh worked at a small restaurant frequented by the city's artists, men who held cigarettes in one hand and the waists of the waitresses in the other. They spoke about glasnost, about liberation, and promised to pay the women later, promised to paint them in the morning, take them somewhere more beautiful than home. Zara remembers Aram, her first lover. This one she remembers simply because he was the first, but there were many who would try to change Zara's life by stealing it, by putting her on paper, putting her in song, putting her in bed, Vardan, Harut, Grigor wrapping her around himself, themselves, all the corners of their country, Andranik and Ruben trying to mold her into something they could understand. They strung her in doorways, buried her and made love to her, and all, all for what? What would've changed what God had carved down in stone: Here stands Zara Manukyan, aged four, forever.

She had seen the mandarins dancing from the kitchen, seated on the counter as her mother rinsed the rice in the sink. They were like orange bells, the branches dipping and waving from the wind, and she had slid down from her mother's view and raced outside because she just wanted a bite before lunch. At four, she knew what she wanted and went after it. Good thing, too, Zara's husband says, voice gentler now, placing both hands on her hips and thumbing down the skin. When he puts his hands over her, Zara remembers everyone else who had done the same. She pushes her sex toward her husband's face. She says, Coffins waited to be filled in the soccer field where my father and brother once played, where my mother and I once watched. A Yugoslav relief plane crashed on the way to Spitak. Forget ambulances—we were taken away on vans the West Germans used to transport their search dogs.

What are you doing, Zara, her husband asks, frowning now, pushing himself up to rest against the headboard.

She walks to their one window. Outside, America. Nothing, I'm sorry. Outside, nothing.

They are on the third floor of an apartment building in East Hollywood, and when she first saw it, Zara calculated how long it would take her to run down the stairs if she had to. Because there is always a reason. This is what she does now: she calculates. How much he spent to court her, how much the flight to Los Angeles, the cost of the banquet hall, only six tables used—fifty dollars a plate, and some of his guests chose to bring presents instead. But who brings presents to weddings in America? And where did she put them? Four days under metal piping and concrete, there's a chance. Five days, good luck. Or the deejay, or the centerpieces, though Zara's mother-in-law had tried to save money, placed a single lily in the kind of jars she used to store the jam for the winters. Sweets all year long. Small reminder of the mother before Gertha. What was her name?

Don't be nervous, Zara's husband says. We don't have to do this tonight. He pats the mattress like he would a small dog. Please just come back to bed.

Zara's first lover, Aram, painted reclining nudes but drew the eyes with pencil. She thought him charming, brilliant because he could afford to paint for a living and not because he could paint. He would ask the models to lick their index fingers and smear the canvas. She needed the money and so smudged her face to make it look like a mistake. She licked the canvas herself, with her tongue, and she had tasted like her dead brother, sunflower seeds, her father's glass of champagne, her mother rotting in her mouth. She kept licking until the paper was wetted through, until it crinkled, almost ripped. Aram told her that her paintings would sell for much, much more than those of the other girls, and she had opened her legs for him because she was told that's what you did when someone tells you you're special. You let someone fill you with their confidence. You make them make you believe it.

"Can you paint my face," she asked in the morning, though what she wanted to see was her forehead, just to see what was written there, once and for all.

"Darling, I smudge faces because if I didn't, the buyers would. What matters is the body. Your body. You, here, now. Who cares what's up there?"

And then, to stop the tears, she began to hum one of Gertha's songs, or her real mother's, she couldn't quite recall; only the melody, only the music was true. Aram was inspired. He sent her down the street to a musician friend from the restaurant. "Maybe Levon can help you," he said. He didn't look at her face when he said it, but that didn't matter because her eyes were closed anyway. Just keep taking what God wants you to take, Zara, because He has taken you into his Hand.

Zara, Zara, where are you, her husband calls out, his voice high and strained. And she knows that this isn't easy for him, either. But it is easier.

Here, she says, and turns away from the window, returns to him, bends on the carpet, folds her arms on the bed to rest her head on her hands. She feels the pressure of her heels against her buttocks. Before, she used to pray like this. If your knees hurt, then God's listening. God's letting you know He's there. God knows you're serious. Stupid saying, but Gertha said it sounded better in German, like everything else. Zara used to pray for sweets from Papa, for Gokor to stop pushing her when no one was looking, for Mama to kiss her more often under the chin, but she remembers something else now, something more real, the sound of her mother's laugh as she twists herself into a brassiere. Beauty is pain, she had said. But Zara has learned that for men this is different. It is the other way. Things get lost in translation, Armineh had warned her as Zara packed her bags for Los Angeles. O, lovely Armineh, who had months before gone away to New York but then was returned to Yerevan after the wedding. Ruined, her almost-husband had discovered, in a way that was undeniable, visible and red.

You know, I'm lucky to have found you, Zara's husband says, sitting with his legs open and caressing her cheek. Zara nods because she is naked in front of yet another man who has promised her something different.

Zara met him, this winning ticket, her American-born Armenian husband, when she was taking her break at work. She was smoking a cigarette, a habit picked up from Aram and reinforced by the others, watching the ducks on the lake beside the restaurant go round and round, soundless in the dark. It was a small lake. Manmade. And it was cold. She wasn't wearing a jacket because sometimes the patrons would offer, because for many men, Zara was an education. What did she do for a living, the American immigration officer had asked Zara. She went from body to body identifying the dead. I am the town historian, she answered.

By that manmade lake, Zara took the cigarette from her mouth and aimed it long, steady and true. It landed just centimeters from a young duck, who stared at the floating stick for barely a second before taking it into her yellow mouth and swallowing it whole.

"A little cruel of you," the man who would be her husband said, voice coming from behind, but she wasn't startled. She had seen him seated with an English newspaper and vodka, pretending to be there accidentally, like he didn't know what this place was, tired from a business trip, or jaded from vacationing in the city his parents were born in. But his glass was still full, he was still on the front page, and even from where she was standing, she noticed his eyes—his eyelashes, so long they cast a shadow on his cheeks, and she thought he looked so different, suddenly and stupidly, from everyone else. This is how it always happens.

"I've been working here for a long time, and that stupid duck still hasn't learned not to eat anything I throw at it."

"That doesn't make it any less cruel," he said, taking a sip, his eyes on her.

Zara reaches over to kiss them now. With eyes closed, everyone looks the same, dead or living. I just need a minute, she tells her husband. Maybe five, maybe ten. She smiles with her teeth showing. Maybe a bath. Of course, he says. Hot water all year round. He laughs, and it's a little mean, a little too sincere, like him. Welcome to America. I won't be long, she says, and resists the urge to lock the bathroom door behind her. Welcome to marriage.

The cold seeps from the floor tiles and into her bones, and Zara curls her toes under her feet as she reaches across the tub to turn on the water. She walks back to the door, presses her ear against white paint, hears nothing. Perhaps he is asleep, she thinks. Perhaps this is all a dream.

She bends to touch her ankles, reaches to touch the sky, waits for the tub to fill, the water to rise. She doesn't take out the sewing needle she has hidden in her makeup case, but if she did, it would be the thumb, she has decided. If not tonight, then tomorrow, or the next. So much time ahead of Zara. The most sensitive, quickest finger to bleed, that odd little thing, veering away from all the others, always. Her husband would not notice. Only the bloodied sheet in the morning, and then she could finally start living.

Zara steps inside the tub, lets herself slide, completely submerging herself in bathwater. She doesn't try opening her eyes, like she used to as a child, when she wanted to see what the world looked like when she was down below it. When she can't hold her breath any longer, Zara emerges, gasping. The blood rushing to her head is a sea between her ears. Zara does it again and again, sinking and rising, liking how the water fills her nose and ears and everything.

Unfair, all the ways she had prettied herself for her husband this evening, Zara thinks, brushing her hair slick back against her scalp, and here he is still long-lashed and beautiful. Her second bath of the day. Her insides smell like pomegranate and passion-fruit, she has washed herself so thoroughly. If he puts his tongue deep into her, he might find her, but who is looking for anything alive amidst all the rubble?

Her husband's first wife had cut him when he was sleeping, just took it to his chin and carved a line down like a surgeon saving someone. She had slept with another man and he wanted her gone, so early morning, she cut him. She cried as he threw her against the wall, wrestled the blade from her hands. And do you know what she said, the man who would become Zara's husband had asked her, drinking his vodka, watching her shiver by the water, watching her watch the duck. She said my chin was too heavy on her chest, that she felt as if I was crushing her when I leaned over her body to kiss her face.

There is a knock on the bathroom door, then the click of the knob turning, and Zara is surprised by how embarrassed she is, how she raises her knees and tries to cover herself.

He leans against the doorway, whistles. My beautiful wife.

She blushes, looks away. Perhaps she is becoming what she needs to be after all to survive. Embarrassed. I am embarrassed, can he tell? Did I finally get it right?

But no, Zara. There was no snow the day of the earthquake. Why did you run? What made you leave your mother's side? What made you leave her? No snow to weigh down the branches of the mandarin tree. You were picking bruised fruit from the ground when the first quake hit, and the sugar mill where your father worked exploded, sending clouds of white, of pulverized seed, across all of Spitak.

Zara starts shaking, and the water splashes around her. Armineh survived when her house collapsed fifteen kilometers away in Kirovakan because she was bathing. Something strong about bathtubs. As long as she stays here, she is safe, and she doesn't know who else is, too, so they are all safe.

Zara, her husband says, bending to one knee, not unlike when he proposed to his first wife, not unlike his second at all. We don't have to do this tonight. You are beautiful, kind. I can be kind too. He laughs. I can wait.

She wants him to make her believe it. But he was not even her first suitor from Los Angeles. Kind, she thinks, trying to catch her breath. Like the giving type. Zara remembers rugs with impossible colors and shapes, patterns she may have understood once, like relics. She had given the world. The water is cold. No, she will put a new rug on the wall, have it hang over their marriage bed.

Where can we buy rugs, she asks him, standing, and he tumbles back, falls on his elbows. She peers at him as she rubs down her knees, though there is only the expectation of an ache there and not the real thing. Still, it counts if you feel it, yes? Something hovering above the bone, the skin? Rugs, he asks, raising an eyebrow, taking another step, reaching for her hip. You mean like IKEA? IKEA, she repeats, liking how the word forms in her mouth. She loved languages. Witch, witch, witch, the world began to whisper when they saw her with the soldiers, the Americans, the Italians, smiling beside Gorbachev, smiling because that's what you did when the man behind the big, black camera says, Little girl, aren't you happy to be alive? The orphanage was a relief, though the whispers followed her there, too. The only living girl in Spitak. You're famous, the ladies brushing her hair told her. Don't let it go to your head. Years later, she returned to Spitak because she just could not stay away any longer. Because she had begun to forget the taste of mandarins, the burst of citrus filling her nose and stinging the insides. Everything tasted like nothing. Because that's what you did when you didn't know what you were doing: you went home.

Remember when you were happy that I was alive, she wanted to knock on the doors of every one of their houses and ask them. But she did not ask, she did not knock. There were no streets, Zara whispers, and steps out of the bathtub. Her husband scrambles to rise, to understand his Armenian wife. No houses. No doors. The whole city, gone. What was left when I left was gone. I was screaming at nothing. I was opening my mouth, I was making room for something, but what was there to taste but my heart?

And the mandarin tree, he asks, his voice softer, and Zara thinks that this is not too bad. Isn't marriage like this, regardless of who you marry? Just having someone ask you the questions that people have always asked you, but with a softer voice? I couldn't remember where it was, she says, taking his hand, curling it around her breast. Maybe it was there, maybe I walked past it and didn't recognize it. She smiles at him. Was I silly to expect a plaque? Here stood Zara Manukyan, aged four, when the world did not stand.

My first wife is pregnant with another man's child. To new beginnings, Zara's husband says, because he can't help himself, he was born here. He is always looking forward. He is not turning his head back to wink. He is lowering his head, flicking his tongue over his second wife's nipple.

The other children in the country who survived the earthquake did not fare better, Zara says, looking down to see that she is dripping on his toes. I was lucky, she says. She tosses her head back and forth to dry her hair. He takes two steps back, grimacing, putting up his hands like she could hurt him. Still, and always, the luckiest. I have you, she says, and wants to mean it. Hours before at the church, for their vows, they had touched foreheads, like they still do in Armenia. But she had thought it would be different here. Perhaps to kiss him there in the church, that would've blessed them, would've changed the taste stuck in her throat. Grief lives on the tongue, Armineh had told her before Zara walked out of the apartment they shared in Yerevan, dragging her suitcase behind her. So just swallow it. Close your eyes and just swallow.

Zara walks toward her husband, past him. Sits on the edge of the mattress, the water pooling down her spine, into the crevices of her back, darkening the sheet.

Is it so stupid that Zara thought it would be different now in this bed, their first night as lovers, with a man who, in his own small, American ways, too had suffered? Just kiss him, she tells herself, but she keeps moving her mouth in a different direction.

Don't cry, he tells her, getting down on his knees, kissing her knees. But she's not, she never really was, never really has. No proof of that here on her skin or anywhere else. It's just my face, she says. No proof of her anywhere at all. And my face, he asks, taking her hand and letting it drape over his nose and eyes. What do you see in my face?

These intimate games, she thinks. They are all the same, deceptive things we do in the dark.

Aram's friend from the restaurant, Levon, was a pianist, and he had no qualms playing her as he would any other beautiful thing. So she let him. He only drank white wine and she thought him complicated. He was not unkind, but he had other girls. One night he asked her to kiss his cousin, a quiet, skinny girl with a gap between her teeth who lived with him, who lived with them. One could never hear her coming, her steps were so gentle and light, and Zara would jump whenever she appeared beside her.

"I'm going to call my next sonata Sisters," Levon said, waving his hands and twirling around them like a zealous conductor. "My double inspirations!" But Zara already had her starring role, and she would not play a supporting part. Zara bit that girl's tongue, though she had wanted to bite off Levon's head instead.

"Don't you know who I am," she screamed at them. "Don't you know I am the only one? Don't you know that it is just me, just me, and nobody else?"

Your face is of comfort, Zara tells her husband, looking not at him, but at the mirror-door behind. You don't look like anyone I know, she tells her reflection. She takes her husband's head into her hands, touches his scar with her nose, and kisses it. Almost there, she thinks. She has found something here, so far from everything else. Just swallow, she tells herself, and asks instead, Do you think we are in love? Because she remembers, no, that she is not kind. She is a witch. In dark waters, she could light an animal on fire.

Zara's husband pushes himself from her, stands. I asked you if you wanted a chance to start fresh. I asked you if you could be happy, and could be happy with me. And do you remember your answer, Zara? She crosses her legs and then uncrosses them. She puts her hand over her dark shape, but it feels so stupid to pretend that she is not naked here, in front of her husband, in a city where no one has seen her without her head.

Zara says, I said give me a reason to leave.

You said give me a reason to live.

Tell me why you chose me, she begs, grabbing his neck, thrusting her tongue in his mouth, pressing it against one canine and then the other, wanting it to slice through. Please, just slice through. Let me taste something I can recognize. But he pushes her away, and Zara retreats back to the small corner of the world that is hers, the edge of the bed.

And then there was Mikael. Mikael who was no artist, no actor, no one pretending to understand. Mikael who made shoes for a living, who sat in a factory room with ninety-nine other men and pounded leather against wood. Mikael who had wrestled in youth, whose ears were sewed to his scalp, who walked hunched over, ready, waiting. Who had stopped by the restaurant because he just wanted a glass of water, he said, he was feeling so warm. I feel like I am on fire, he said, and she lifted the glass to his mouth and nursed him back to health, cooled him down with the strength of her own miraculous body. God, she thought, there. There. He is the one. He is the reason why I am here. He is why. If not for him, then who? If not for a person, then what?

Tell me why you wanted me, Zara begs her husband, standing. Look at me. Tell me why I stood out. Why me?

But these things are different, aren't they? For men and women? Mikael had a wife. He didn't try to hide it when he took her home. So she took this, too, the stupid duck. Afterward, when he went to wash up, Zara walked from room to room, naked and sticky, and she licked everything. The sharp edges of a Romeo and Juliet figurine on top of the fireplace mantle, the warm, pickled tomatoes sinking in their yellow water, the framed photo of him and his wife holding their two daughters.

Mikael caught her by the door, mouth pressed against the knob, down on her knees. "I used to pray like this," she said when he asked her what she was doing.

You didn't stand out, Zara, her husband says, grabbing her hips and bringing her to him. I love you, he says, looking at her through his beautiful lashes. But back then I was so lost, I was so hurt, I would've picked anyone. I could have married any one of you.

THE KINGSLEY DRIVE CHORUS

On the corner of Kingsley and De Longpre, we lived our lives pressed against the glass. Our husbands—carpenters, jewelers, mechanics and slaves—spent their days without us. When they came home in the evenings, they were quiet, and so we were quiet, too. Our children retreated into worlds that were unkind to us, the girls into schoolbooks with words beyond our knowing and our boys onto the winding streets of Los Angeles. We had done what we could, all the things we told ourselves we could have done. We resigned ourselves to our windows. We wiped down the glass. We waved hello and goodbye.

The first time Zaven called her from jail, Carmen Oganesyan did what any of us would do: she blamed his friends. She told us she had a feeling when he first introduced Robert and Vardan to her, all those years ago. They were Mariam's boys. They lived in #3. The Oganesyans were in the back of the building, in #12, new tenants as well as new Americans. Robert and Vardan were a little too skinny in the arms, like they hadn't lifted a single weight in their entire lives. And their spiked hair, curving slightly inwards, made the brothers look like they were constantly being pulled forward despite their will. Robert, at fifteen, was a tall boy who tried hard not to be. He wore oversized sweaters and pants that added bulk to his thin frame, and slouched when he walked. We all thought he'd have back troubles by the time he was thirty, but he found himself with bigger problems much earlier. Vardan was a quiet child, thirteen, Zaven's age when the Oganesyans moved in, but his quietness made us uncomfortable. You'd say hello as you passed him in the garden, carrying your groceries, and he'd glance down at your heavy plastic bags and say absolutely nothing. These were not the kind of boys Carmen wanted her Zaven to befriend, but she felt satisfied that he was at least making an attempt to fit in, to return to the happy life that she and her husband had pulled him out of in Yerevan just months before.

When Zaven called, Carmen was in the kitchen, preparing her famous *kyoftas*. Just imagine little eggs of beef, filled with more beef. They taste great with a squeeze of lemon. New Year's Eve was approaching, and we were all busy making the same food and hoping they'd taste different, better than everyone else's. But no one could make *kyoftas* like Carmen. She had beautiful hands. After dipping her long fingers into the bowl of cold water, she'd mold the ground mixture into a shell, thumbing the beef and bulgur into place. The shells were thin, but never broke, and she'd stuff them with filling before closing them, always leaving an exaggerated tip on top that hardened after cooked. Everyone broke off that piece first. She'd joke that to make the perfect *kyofta* you'd have to pretend that it was a child's head you were washing. You had to be careful, certainly, but more than that, you had to do it with love. The egg always knows, she'd say. Like self-destruction was an accusation of neglect, a threat carried out, excusable. Perhaps.

Only eighteen, Zaven was out on bail the next day. Carmen was a proud woman, but not enough to let him stay in jail. She asked us for loans, a hundred dollars here, a hundred there. Some of us helped; most couldn't. All of us, even those without sons, sympathized. Our boys don't adapt well here. Something doesn't translate well. We don't worry much about the girls because they're beautiful and smart and quick to assimilate. Like Armineh's daughter, Sona, going to Berkeley now, a good enough reason to leave her mother alone with a finicky husband all year long. Or Sofia, Ruzan's oldest. We hear she's married and has a kid, a beachfront house in San Diego, a White husband. We don't have many success stories here that star our boys.

Carmen said her son would be different. But we told her that sons become not their fathers, or even their grandfathers, but something altogether terrible. And we can't help but love them because they are ours, though it is hard to do. Carmen said that this was the problem, that our love stopped becoming easy, and what is a boy to turn into but a monster if his mother does not see in him a God? It was drugs. He was found smoking marijuana in the bathroom stalls of the community college with Robert and Vardan. Vardan, just months shy of being legal, got away with a reprimand. Robert and Zaven were charged and then eventually released after a few hours due to overcrowding. Carmen met her son outside of the jail. Mariam wasn't there, so Carmen hugged her son, too.

Back then, we didn't go to Mariam's for coffee or *gata*. We were polite but Mariam flaunted her sons' failures like proof of America's shortcomings, more proud of being right than of anything good or kind her boys had ever done for her. She hadn't wanted to move to Los Angeles. Unlike us, she had lived well in Armenia, but her husband had wanted to live even better. Carmen and Mariam were never friends, but Carmen was the nicest of us. A fault, really, that goodness. Her husband tried to beat it out of her. But she was even better than that, and he knew it, so he stopped once the boy got old. We still don't know if Zaven ever protected his mother, if he ever placed his hand against his father's chest and pushed back. We hope, but we suspect not.

When Zaven came home, Carmen told him to stop spending time with Mariam's sons. They're trouble, she said, they're bringing it into her house.

"Home," Zaven corrected her. "We don't have a house."

"Don't speak to me like that," Carmen replied, putting down the knife and raising a finger. They were sitting on the couch, he sprawled on one end, flipping through channels on the TV, his wife-beater tucked into his track-suit pants. Carmen sat rigidly on the other, peeling a grapefruit, dieting in preparation for the holidays.

"And lower your voice." Carmen put down her hand. "Don't let your father hear you say something stupid like that."

"He's not home," he said, raising his eyebrows. "See what I did there, Ma?"

"Zaven."

Zaven jumped from his seat and grabbed his mother's shoulders. Shook them—with love, Carmen would tell us pointedly—and said, "You're really something, Ma." He kissed her on the forehead and went to his room. He put on Armenian rap, which Carmen hated even more than Black people's rap because she understood every single word. She heard him shut the door and was momentarily flattered by his thoughtfulness, but those lyrics only felt more dangerous now, seeping through the cracks in his door.

Carmen would say hello whenever she'd run into Mariam in the basement laundry, or in the cement backyard where we all hung our linens, not trusting the cranky machines the manager installed because of a complaint to City Council. (He found the cheapest washer at Sears in punishment, and we kept to our bathroom sinks and tubs.) Whenever Mariam's sheets were dry but still on the lines, Carmen would fold them, put them in her own basket and return them to her, knocking softly on the door. Mariam would take them in with a quick nod of the head, biting onto the cigarette so she could use both of her hands. Mariam was not very womanly, no. She was skinny, but not fashionably, her legs so straight that they looked like arms, and she, this strange, hungry creature, always puffing on something. No hips on her, either, not even a hint. Who knew how she gave birth—if she did, at all. We used to talk of adoption. Mariam spent all her time in malls, trying on designer dress after designer dress, pretending she could still buy them.

Carmen didn't fault this in Mariam; she, too, sometimes wished she was someone else, but we believed the problem with Mariam was that she didn't just stop there, with wishing. She didn't live here, with the rest of us, but in her head, with her sad grandeur and delusions of past lives. Carmen was nice, she was polite, but she was no friend to Mariam. Their boys were, however.

Robert and Vardan were just babies when they got to our building. We remember pink, wet lips and fat cheeks, games of tag with older boys who left their mothers hurting as soon as they learned to drive. They were seven and nine, starting elementary school at Ramona. The first few weeks Mariam would walk the mile to school with them, to and from, and we all sighed, remembering ourselves. But it was not long before Mariam let the kids go by themselves. When they returned home, they'd return with bags of chips, with orange fingers or crumbs stuck in their teeth or spotting their white uniforms.

Carmen did her best following the first arrest to break the boys up, and we were all very impressed by her efforts. She'd hide his cellphone, the charger, his wallet, and he'd be so frustrated by the time he found them that he didn't even try to go out. She feigned illnesses, headaches and strange stomach pains, guilted him into staying in. And whenever Robert and Vardan knocked on her door, calling on Zaven, Carmen made sure to answer first, to tell them he was already out, doing whatever it was that young men do. "I'm sure he meant to invite you two," she'd sometimes whisper. "I'm sure you'll run into him somewhere." But there are only so many times a woman can open the door first, anxious and eager. When Carmen explained herself to her suspicious husband, she was met with laughter, a wave of the hand, a "let the boys be boys." But her son was no longer a boy. She couldn't remember the moment he stopped being one, but Carmen knew that only a man could break his mother's heart like that, getting arrested, in a school, no less. Boys know their boundaries.

"Even if he is your son," we told her over coffee, "he's no longer your child."

So, we'd see them together, Zaven, Robert and Vardan. Smoking in front of the 99 Cent Store on Sunset, or the nearby Water Station, at the Shell, smoking as they washed Robert's Camry every other day during summer, making use of the quarters their mothers were supposed to be using for the washer; we'd see them smoking by the main door of the apartment building, huddled in leather jackets, zipped up to their chins. Everywhere we looked, there they were, the three of them, an omen hanging above their heads, so much dark smoke.

*

On August 14, 1998, just hours before she saw her son on television, his head being pushed down into the back of a police car, Carmen was listening to Celine Dion and doing laundry. We all knew whenever she and her husband fought because Dion's songs would reach our ears before word came from her own mouth. She was the prettiest of us, but where we come from, pretty faces are as useless as our husbands' vows of loyalty.

Carmen's hair fell across her chest as she bent down to pick up her son's wet T-shirt from the basket and draped it over the line. Her hair was long and thick, a cascade of dark waves swelling wildly over her breast and into her waist, thinning out at the edges over her hips. Her husband had married her for her hair, she once said. "I kept it in two long braids as a girl and when he first saw me, he just knew he wanted to pull apart those braids, comb them through with his own fingers." But it was hard to imagine Ruben having such a romantic notion. He was a factory-man, tall, with wide, strong shoulders and a thick neck, built to be a laborer. When he came home from work, he still glowed from the heat he faced all day forging metal into iron. His skin was freckled, as if burned by years of walking against the wind. Carmen's description. She really loved him, poor girl, but when has love ever saved anyone?

Carmen's jeans were of a faded blue and they were loose around her stomach, the pouch of lost fat wrinkling unattractively under her top as she bent down to grab another shirt. She had been dieting again, which meant our building smelled for days entirely of cabbage. Carmen was an optimist, a master negotiator. It was an art, the way she tried to appease her husband and keep her son on the right path. She did so many things very well. She had learned, she said, to adapt.

"It's what four years of engineering school teaches you," she told us. "There is always a solution to the problem."

As the years passed, Carmen had figured out just how much salt to put into lentil soup, what shoes Ruben wore most and needed the most shining, when she could wear a skirt and when not. Carmen had graduated from the Civil Engineering Institute of Vanadzor, and married Ruben three weeks later because that's what you did. She found a way to put her education to use, she said.

Unlike his mother, Zaven was a poor student. Disinterested, his mother would clarify, definitely not dumb. He was still going to LACC—going, a relative term, that. Carmen would add, But I know he wants to go to UCLA. He can only take night-classes right now because of work. Another funny word for our children. Thinking that sitting in front of a computer and finding cheap auto parts on Ebay and selling it to local shops was work. Work was what their fathers did, coming home with soot under their nails, sweat under their arms, and money in their pockets. We never saw any of our children's earnings. None of their earnings fed us, put new linens under our bodies, towels that did not leave their pink and blue threads on our damp skins. "As long as Zaven takes care of his expenses, I'm happy," Carmen claimed. We knew otherwise. We knew Carmen wondered just exactly what those expenses were. We certainly did. What does a twenty-one year old without a car, without rent, have to pay off?

Carmen was clipping her wash down when Mariam approached with her own basket. We watched from our living room windows as she put it down by her feet, reached into her dress pocket for a lighter. Carmen's shoulders must've tensed. Since the first arrest three years prior, Carmen had begun to reconsider some of her kindness to Mariam.

We watched as Mariam leaned against the stone wall that blocked in the building's backyard and began taking long drags of her cigarette. Carmen moved her basket slightly to the left and continued her work. She threw a white bed-sheet across the line and pulled it straight. As she bent to pick up the clothespins, she could smell Mariam's cigarette. We saw the face she made from the third floor, and we knew that she wouldn't be able to hold it in much longer.

"Mariam, please."

"What?" Mariam moved her cigarette away from her face and tapped it in the air. "What?"

Carmen pointed at the cigarette. "The sheets, Mariam."

"Excuse me?"

Carmen shook her head and kicked again her basket to the left, a little harder this time. The plastic container scraped against the concrete until it touched the trunk of the tired fig tree. Our only source of joy sometimes, this, peeling away the sticky skin for a taste of home.

"Do you not understand why I don't want smoke on my sheets?"

"Don't be dramatic. It's one little cigarette. I'm not doing a goddamn barbeque."

"That's the problem with you, Mariam. One cigarette is enough to stain a whole load."

"Problem with me?" Mariam put the cigarette in her mouth and began pulling the wash out of her basket, throwing it on the lines, one on top of the other, until the line dragged, slumping in the middle with the weight.

Carmen didn't say anything as she reached to grab the towel hanging dangerously low. She threw it over her shoulder and continued removing the rest of her wash from the line, a pair of jeans, a few shirts and pillowcases. We shivered thinking about the cold she was bound to get, the wet clothes sinking through the flimsy fabric of her dress and into her bones. She had been complaining about her hands recently, how sometimes she could not make a fist. We told her it was the weather, but we knew it as signs of aging. We told her to dress more warmly.

"Don't worry. God won't let your sheets get dirty. The whole world might end." Mariam laughed and spread the wash across the line, balancing the weight. She didn't look at Carmen, so we did. She seemed so small under all those clothes, her head a little fixture, dimming against the rising whiteness on her shoulders.

Carmen lifted her elbow and placed her palm on top of the left pile, bending with her knees to grab the half-empty basket and put it against her hip. Walking slowly, quietly, she moved past Mariam, and Mariam turned her head to watch her neighbor disappear into our building. Then she spit the cigarette, stomping it out. She lit another, and we watched her smoke it for a while.

*

When she got home, Carmen decided to take a bath. She told us later that she had draped the wash over her furniture, scattering them all around, though she left the undergarments for her bedroom, as they were private business, even if it meant she had to dampen the bed. Ruben liked a clean bed, no frills, just white sheets, good quality, and a pillow for each, but apparently that day he had complained about the breakfast she had made him, that the eggs were too runny, and so she draped her clammy panties and his briefs all over the covers in punishment. She described the scene to us as a little absurd. Sexy, too, a little, she admitted, and we wondered when she had last performed her wifely duties. It made her blush as she looked at her work—we could picture this so clearly, her rosy cheeks, the color bruising her neck, too. Sometimes Carmen's passion was stronger than her sense of decency, but we knew God would forgive her for that. It wasn't often.

When she returned to the bathroom, she said the heat warmed her bones with promise. In Yerevan where they had lived, the water came on at two in the morning and the Russians shut off the gas five minutes before that. (Our friends, the Russians. How dreadful to admire someone so fiercely and have them hate you in return). Each day, each night, they had water for exactly fifteen minutes. Some of us remember this, sitting in the darkened living room, waiting to hear the deep rumbling of water course through our brick walls and pulse below our feet. We'd hurry to the bathroom to pick up the pots and pitchers stacked on the floor and fill them from the faucet, filling as much as she could before it all stopped.

The day the Soviet Union fell, Ruben started planning their way out, and she was grateful. America meant one thing for Carmen: that Zaven would not have to bathe at night, in freezing temperatures, with buckets of water. That she wouldn't have to look down at Zaven sleeping on his stomach, his feet digging into the mattress, the sheets pooled under his chest, and shake him awake. If Carmen was awake now in the middle of night, it was not because she had work to do, water to collect. It was because she wanted to look at Zaven asleep, see his face soften, his eyebrows, slightly touching in the middle, unfurrowed. Carmen used to imagine taking a razor to the soft area between his eyes, pushing down the blade against his skin quickly in his sleep, so as not to wake him, so as not to let him know that he was not perfect.

After Carmen rinsed herself and stepped out of the bathroom, she was surprised to hear sirens blaring. She wrapped the robe closely around her as she moved to the kitchen window. Carmen craned her heard over the sink, her forehead pushing against the thin screen. Police cars weren't rare on Kingsley Drive, but they weren't common in the afternoon. At night, we knew things happened, that people got hurt, did things they regretted in the morning.

Carmen couldn't see much, but when she heard the helicopter, so close that the palm trees on our street trembled and whistled in the air, she felt as if she, too, were fluttering away. She hurried to her door and locked it. She clutched at her robe, then dropped her hands to her side, scolding herself. She walked toward the home phone, taking measured breaths. When she dialed his number, she didn't expect Zaven to pick up. Like us, she always had to try her son several times so he could know that she was serious, that it was not just another motherly call, a how are you doing or where are you now? She clicked the red button and dialed again, punching in the numbers one by one instead of pressing redial. "To give him time," she'd explain. At the third attempt, she moved towards the window again, and Carmen saw all of us making our way towards the main building gate door, walking slow and talking fast. She saw us trying to get a closer look. Later, when she asked us what we thought we'd see out there, why we left our apartments, why we weren't afraid, we told her the truth: because our sons had either picked up their phones or were already in jail. When you know that your children are safe—even there, even there they can be safe, safer—you grow bold. Relief makes you do foolish things.

Carmen turned away from us. She moved the damp t-shirts from the couch and took a seat on the cold leather. She picked up the television remote, hoping for something funny. But there, on Channel 7, breaking news, her little boy, looking not very little at all, taking up the backseat of a police car, his face covering, it seemed, the whole window. He was looking straight at her with the kind of expression Carmen always tried to convince herself was learned, something he had picked up from his angry friends, something not natural to his face. Carmen took one of the wet shirts beside her, brought it to her face and screamed.

*

The Armenian Channel did a special broadcast a week later. We all watched. Mr. Levon Hagopyan sat behind his fancy desk, hands clasped as in church, and talked into the camera and our living rooms. "Women," he said. "Women, you need to do something. We have had enough. Enough of these shipwrecked boys, losing their way in Los Angeles. They're in prisons, in unhappy marriages, in motel bathrooms by the 101 highway, shooting up. They're your sons. Just what are you going to do about it?" We watched him shaking his head in disgust and we nodded along. It pains us to admit this, to remember.

After the arrest, the only time we saw Carmen was in the backyard, hanging her wash, the snap of the line as she jerked her linens off. We'd glance out of our window from time to time and she appeared to us smaller than ever, smaller than before, much smaller still.

Mr. Levon Hagopyan told us that police had responded to an anonymous phone call. The caller noticed three men entering a house on Kentwood, from the back, dressed in dark clothes and wearing sunglasses. The house was of an elderly Armenian couple, and they were home when they weren't supposed to be. They were tied with masking tape. The Sulemanyans sat with hands behind their backs on their maroon couches, waiting, watching as three boys that looked like they could one day marry their granddaughters ransacked their house. When they heard the sirens, the boys ran to the car. Robert drove, his brother beside him, Zaven in the back. Robert drove for three miles before he nicked a Sedan with two children and a mother inside. "The police report tells us," Mr. Levon Hagopyan said, "that the Sedan spun twice and then slammed into an oncoming Nissan. The youngest broke his arm and the mother now wears a scar on her forehead." On Western, the Camry scraped a parked truck, and the police behind the boys multiplied. The helicopter caught up. Then the boys thought to make a run for it, in the daytime, with the helicopter above them and the police behind. They decided to run home. They were running to us. In front of our very steps, on Kingsley Drive, the police caught them. Vardan and Robert were brought down together because they were running just inches apart. Zaven met the pavement by himself. The cameraman caught the moment. As she waited for her husband to come home, Carmen watched the news, all of it, every channel. She took one of Ruben's taped movies and recorded over it, a good fifteen minutes. And always of the same scene, that second when Zaven looks behind him, twisting his neck, and the officers press their palms into his face and push him down onto the gravel. And the moment after, when Zaven looks out of the police car window, the cameras flashing him a ghastly white.

*

We don't know where Mariam was when her boys got taken away, if she was hiding in her apartment, or hiding from herself, but we saw her the next day, sitting on the low stoops in front of her place. Her head was wrapped in a towel and a tattered robe revealed her purple-veined legs. She was smoking, head tilted back, breathing in the same smoke she breathed out. There was a plate of chocolate cake next to her, a gold-plated fork stabbed into its center. But the cake appeared untouched. When she saw us noticing it, she picked it up with her free hand and waved it at in our faces.

"You want it? Take it."

We shook our heads.

"Take it. I'm not going to eat it. I thought I might, but I'm not hungry."

"Mariam," we said.

"Fuck you. I said take it. You want my fucking cake? Take it and don't feel bad about it. Take it home and share it."

"Mariam," we pleaded. But she blew the smoke in our faces, and we turned away as if slapped. When we caught her eyes once more, she was chewing wildly, her whole face contorted, cheeks puffed out and nose flaring, brown smearing her upper lip.

A month later, Carmen and Mariam had a talk. We tried not to listen in, not to open our windows just a crack, because we understood how easy it was to destroy the illusion of dignity between broken women. We did it anyway because we were hurting too. We had rooted for Carmen, for her boy, for ourselves. Even when we stopped, we like to tell ourselves now, we didn't. Mariam had just taken out the trash when Carmen turned the corner with her basket. The women stopped short of running into each other, but the space between them was like no space at all. They stood there for a second before Carmen moved the basket from her hip to her stomach, and Mariam took a step back.

"Yes, yes, that's right. You do that. You keep going, Mariam. And don't stop until you're miles away from here."

Mariam laughed, and we cringed. Her laugh could be a bitter thing, as if it scraped her throat as it rose from her belly.

"Don't be silly, Carmen. It's not very becoming. What would your husband say if he saw that ugly expression on your face?"

Carmen put down her basket, bending slowly in front of Mariam, and for a moment we worried that Mariam would push her down, shove Carmen into that little plastic container that seemed to be forever attached these days to her thinning shape. But it was Carmen who made us gasp as she took a wet blouse from the basket and flung it at Mariam's face. Mariam whipped her head back, but the shirt seemed to fix itself around her, wrapping its sleeves around her ears. Mariam pulled it off with the tips of her fingers, dropping it to her side like it was a dirty diaper.

"You're pathetic." Mariam whispered it so softly we thought we misheard, we pushed our heads closer against our windows. Carmen pulled her arm back, but she didn't strike. Mariam only tilted her head to the side and looked at her.

"Can't you see what you've done?"

Mariam looked behind her, then turned back. She placed a hand over her chest. "Me?"

Upstairs we wanted to nod along. We wanted to point. Now the whole world knew what we knew, what we learned here. That we loved our sons not because of who they were, but because of what they were to us.

Carmen put down her hand, kept both hands rigid to her side, fingers pointed straight. She looked like a solider. She looked like someone who could fly. "How can you just stand there? How can you pretend none of this has happened? How can—"

"All you do is ask questions, Carmen. Questions, questions, questions. Why me? Well, why the hell not?"

"Why were you never at the trials?"

Mariam put her hands over her face and groaned. But then her groan turned into a strained laughter muffled by skin, like she was convulsing. Carmen frowned, took a step forward. But when Mariam removed her hands, her teeth showed. "Because I know what my boys are. I don't need the court to tell me."

"And what are they, Mariam?"

"They're worthless."

The slap stunned us. The suddenness of Carmen's movement, the loudness of the flat thud. We jerked from the windows, out of breath, and just as quickly, moved back. Mariam very slowly righted her neck. She licked her lips and we shook our heads. From above, we mouthed a plea: stay silent.

"They're criminals."

Carmen slapped her again, her palm hitting the same side of Mariam's face. An audible sigh escaped Mariam's mouth, a distant echo of relief. We began to pound on the glass. Carmen kept her hand in the air. The women didn't look up.

"I wish they weren't mine."

There are a few things we remember of that moment. The sound Carmen's knees made as she hit the ground, like the logs our fathers would axe in the mornings during the summer months, when they were split open and fell on opposite sides. The way Mariam looked down at Carmen, the gentle shake of the head, and the way she looked up at us, leaning back, her hands brushing the hair from her face, eyes unblinking. How she stepped over Carmen's basket and her outstretched arms. Carmen, there on the ground, bent forward like a Turk, wailing. And when we averted our eyes, resting them on our empty couches, the feeling we used to get when we were young girls, our backs opening once a month, that gnawing feeling all over, like little kernels pushing against the skin, ready to puff up, ready to burst, but never gathering enough heat, enough steam, always missing the opportunity to become something beautiful.

*

In the following weeks, Carmen seemed to return to her former self. She smiled when we saw her outside, checking the mail, she winked when we caught her cutting the basil that grew by her stoops—our landlord forbid it, said the smell hid other smells—pocketing them swiftly in the money pouch she wore around her waist when she was gardening. She came over for coffee, for stories. We tried not to pry but Carmen appeared comfortable sharing with us the details of how she found out, what she was feeling, how her son was doing. We weren't too surprised; we were like that, too, finding comfort in the telling. It saddened us, disappointed us, but her acceptance of the situation was of great solace, too. She was not any better than us.

Of course, some things we knew we could never ask. What Ruben thought about all this. What Zaven had to say. Just what he was going to plead. Some questions are not so much questions as they are accusations. We were careful. We couldn't help it. We had our friend Carmen back and we tried to forget about Mariam, the way she looked up at us that day, all-knowing and unapologetic. Carmen didn't mention her name.

The holidays were approaching and we went to work. We buttered our filo doughs and ground our walnuts. We chopped up our carrots, pickles and potatoes and put them in the back of the refrigerators. We took out the beef to thaw and rinsed out the bulgur. We unearthed our fine china and the Italian-made tablecloths left over from our dowries.

When we just came to America, our children tried to force us to celebrate Christmas on the 25th, like their classmates did. But ever since we could remember, we had exchanged presents and drunken kisses and plates of *kyofta* on the 31st. New Years' Eve. It was a Soviet leftover, and one we tried very hard to get our kids to understand. Celebrating the start of a fresh beginning, where the past didn't matter, where the past was just that, past—that still had great meaning for us, especially as immigrants. So the 25th came and passed, and we hurried to the departments stores to do our "Christmas" shopping, taking advantage of all the sales on clothing and ornaments, shirts and shoes and dancing Santas.

Carmen cut down the laundry line on the morning of the 30th. She just took a scissor close to the two poles and snapped it right off. The thin rope fell to the ground, and Carmen bent down and began rolling it loosely around her wrist, like it was merely yarn for the knitting. When she was finished, she looked up at us, and we waved from our windows. She smiled and waved back. It was her normal smile, wide, no teeth showing—she was always embarrassed of her teeth. Did the smile reach her eyes? We women always wash our windows on the 31st, so we can welcome the New Year with light unobstructed, our glass spotless and vision the most clear. On the 30th, we couldn't see as closely.

It was Mariam who found her. Mariam who stood up on the stool that Carmen had used to draw a noose from the drainage pipe in our laundry room. Mariam who had wrapped one arm around Carmen's waist as she cut down the rope ripping into our friend's skin. She who fell under Carmen's body on the dirty ground next to the washing machines. Skinny old Mariam. It was then that she cried out, then when Carmen's body fell on her chest, Carmen's head gently sloping over her pounding heart, that Mariam let out a howl, so terrible, so strange, so loud, that we stopped in our kitchens, in our living rooms, and grabbed at our necks. When we reached the laundry room, Mariam was sitting with her legs spread open, Carmen between them, Carmen with her head back falling over Mariam's shoulder, Mariam rocking back and forth, Mariam shh shh shh-ing, like it was a child in her lap, like Carmen was still alive and only hurting.

*

Ruben didn't tell Zaven that his mother was dead until after the funeral. He served six years, was out early on good behavior. He married quickly, began driving a truck, bought a small one-bedroom condo a few miles from here. As for Robert and Vardan, we don't know much. Mariam tells us that they are free to live their own lives and that her main concern has always been to do the same. Now she says Los Angeles is not such a bad place to grow old in. She waters the fig tree in the backyard and plants a new batch of basil every spring. She takes cooking classes at the community college and invites us over for dessert. Before she takes the first sip of her *surj*, Mariam raises the cup in toast. To all those we have lost, she says.

And knowing what we know now and seeing what we have seen, we can't help but nod. We bring the demitasse cups to our lips and sip soundlessly. But the taste of Mariam's coffee is always bitter. At night, when we return to our apartments, when we put our heads to the pillow, when we lie beside our husbands, we still can't help but wonder. If all it took was for them to see us dead, we too would've done it ourselves.

MILES TO EXIT

When he tells Albert that it's not the boy's fault, Albert agrees and says, "You're right. It's yours." And maybe it is. So three years later, when Albert is gone, it is up to Sarkis Movsepian to teach the boy to drive.

They're sitting in the brown '93 Mazda Albert left behind, in the underground garage of their apartment building, and the light is so low, Sarkis can barely make out his grandson's nose beside him. And it's a big nose. Sarkis touches his own face. He's a tall man, heavyset still, but his face is the face of an old person. He rubs down his bushy eyebrows and licks his lips, forever chapped, dead skin in the corners moving up and down with every word. He is almost seventy. Reassurance was a game he used to play with his wife, but she is dead now. Sarkis takes out his glasses, rubs it with the handkerchief he has carried with him since he was in the Soviet Army, and puts it back on. He blinks rapidly, then flicks on the light.

"Well, the first thing we do is what?" he asks the boy.

But Armen is not like most boys. He is not holding the wheel with both hands and sitting forward. Not brushing his hair back as he looks in the rearview mirror. Not fiddling with the radio, trying to find the music his body is already in motion to. Armen shrugs, twisting in his seat to smile at him. The boy has always had a strange smile. Very thin, disappearing into his face, like he is afraid to bare his teeth. But the boy has good teeth. Strong. Straight. Sarkis knows Armen cleans them with threads, that he gurgles Listerine twice a day, even brushes his tongue. Other boys must also do this, Sarkis thinks, so he does not understand why his grandson does not smile like these other boys, too.

"I put on my seatbelt?" Armen says.

Sarkis frowns. "Is this a question?"

"No."

"Then this is the wrong answer. First important thing!"

"Put the key in?" Armen asks.

"And then you are dead. First thing, you check backseat. Maybe some thief is hiding with a knife in hand."

"East Hollywood's not that great, *Papik*, but it's not Compton. I'll be fine." Armen scratches under his nose. Only fifteen, he has a mustache, narrow and even, as if done by pencil, closely clipped and outlining his upper lip. Sarkis hates it. It makes the boy resemble a cartoon, a strange approximation of a man. He wants to tell the boy there are other ways to prove his masculinity. Driving, for example. The mustache makes him stand out. And sometimes Sarkis worries that this is just what the boy wants, to wear the burden on his face.

He looks at the boy, really looks. Armen is thin and tall, almost two heads above the neighborhood children. He has grown into his limbs, but they still dangle when he walks like someone has broken his bones, like his legs are jelly. The boy does not run. He does not lift weights. He does not swim. He does not, does not. Armen sits. Armen stays. His teachers describe him as nice. And Armen's lashes, the way they reach his dark eyebrows, curling gently into them—it made Albert furious and it made him leave, but it only turns Sarkis quiet now. Armen's eyes are round and large and so brown they're black, but no, Sarkis can see nothing of himself there. Not Albert, not Luisa. Only his wife, his lovely Armenouhi.

"Los Angeles is not City of Angels, boy," he warns Armen.

Sarkis learns his English from police shows and made-for-TV movies with titles that are paired opposites, like *Truth and Lies* or *Love and Lust*. He understands that things in life are not that simple, but life is different in Los Angeles: he is not living here. Most days, he thinks about dying, what a relief it would be, to be with his wife once more.

He pokes at the boy's shoulder, tells him: "Always check behind before reverse. And before reverse, put key in! After key, move this to the R letter."

"And at what point do I put on my seatbelt, *Papik?*" Armen says, tapping his fingers on the steering wheel.

"Funny boy."

Armen's nails are chipped, bitten down, but Sarkis can still see the residue of black marker the boy uses to color them in when on the couch, legs crossed, scribbling letters on his nails. After he stares at it for a while, an arm held straight before him, Armen will put it back on his thigh and fill in all the white space, darkening the nails completely. Sarkis doesn't ask what the boy writes on his body, but he is thankful for his attempts to hide it. The boy must be sensible now. He is almost a man. He needs to take care. He needs to get rid of the mustache.

Sarkis rolls down the window and adjusts the passenger-side door mirror. He has not driven for years because he didn't have to when Albert was around, and now he won't allow himself. His friends in the building, Toshko and Garbis, think him a fool. They tell him, "You stop driving when American DMV tells you stop." But Sarkis feels the weight of his body shift and it scares him. In the mornings, he is heavy, legs numb and tingling, feet dragging on the carpet. At night, he is weightless, closing the windows, even in the heat, afraid he will be blown away. Sarkis can no longer trust his body, so he trusts in the hope that he still knows what is best.

"If you don't become master of this car, how will you go places?"

"Friends?"

"Friends?"

"Friends," Armen repeats, turning his gaze on him.

Sarkis pats down the few strands still left on his pinking head. Luisa tells him to shave, that it makes him look silly and sad, but Sarkis needs something to hold onto do during moments like this. It's why he drank as a young man, why he smoked. He liked having something in his hands, something small he could curl his fingers around. He stopped when he met Armenouhi because she had the kind of hair that kept him busy for days, hands that never left his, a thumb that moved in constant circles against the deep of his palm. Sarkis looks at the boy and thinks. The boy makes him think so much. How can he even wonder about who the boy will wrap his arms around, kiss on the mouth or on the forehead—the way he did to Armenouhi when she was sleeping, sitting, standing—or how the boy will love? How can he even begin to wonder about any of these things if he has to worry about how lonely the boy already is?

"Or I'll walk. Don't worry. I'll live somewhere where you don't need a car to get around. Europe, maybe."

"Oh, my boy. People in Europe come to Los Angeles, and you will go to Europe. What is in Europe? Do you know?"

The boy smiles, tugging at the bottom of his lip, then drops his hand. He leans toward him with his shoulder, nudging his own, like they are old friends. Like this, when Armen is playful, open and earnest, he most resembles Armenouhi, and for a second Sarkis feels a tremendous loss. It gathers in his throat like baby birds, and he swallows.

"Beautiful things, Grandpa. Europe is full of beautiful things."

Sarkis sits back and fiddles with the nub, readjusts the mirror. When he peers at his face, he sees himself, and that's the way it should be. No other reflection but your own. But when the child was born, Sarkis bent forward and grabbed his knees, let out long and wheezing breaths. Months before, the doctor had told that it was to be a girl. When it turned out different, Sarkis should've been happy with the surprise. A boy! Should've laughed, patted his son-in-law on the back, should've kissed his daughter Luisa on the forehead. But Armenouhi had died during the middle of Luisa's pregnancy, and all Sarkis wanted to do was say her name. Just wanted that little piece of her, coming out of him, as close to him as was physically possible now. And poor Luisa, she left the bed in her state and came to him.

"Papa," she said. "Don't be sad. We can still name him after Mama. Doesn't he look like an Armen? Come. Does he not look like an Armen?"

And when he looked at the boy, so red in the face, purple a surprise on his lips, wrapped in that heavy white blanket, Sarkis couldn't help but think that there was a bit of his wife in him still, behind those eyes, perhaps, or in the wrinkles on his forehead.

"Armen?" he asked, and the boy had hiccupped in answer, opened his little mouth and winced out the funny sound. And, O, how it made Sarkis laugh. He laughed and laughed, took the boy in his arms and turned and turned. My love, my love, my love.

Sarkis looks at the boy beside him now and squeezes his knee, taps it twice. Armen places a hand over his.

"*Papik*," he says gently—gently, always too gently—and Sarkis knows he has loved him wrong all this time. A boy like Armen needs a car, a chance to be normal. He grabs Armen's hands and forces them on the wheel, coils his fingers around the leather seam.

"Drive now."

*

They settle into a routine. After school, they practice in the garage, parking, reversing, U-turning in tight corners. They only have an hour or so before the men of the building return from work and their cars fill the vacant spaces. On weekends Sarkis wakes the boy early, and they venture onto the empty Hollywood streets. When the boy tires and starts making stupid mistakes, Sarkis knows it is enough. They park the car and step inside the cool supermarkets on Sunset, roaming the aisles, looking for reduced food items. At Food 4 Less, they find bagels about to expire, or off-brand donuts a day already past their date. They buy both. Armen usually stays in the car if they end up at Ranch Market, and Sarkis doesn't ask why. Armen is not the kind of boy who has enemies, but he is the kind of boy people like to make theirs. When they get home, Luisa is already up and squeezing oranges into juice.

A month into their lessons, Sarkis tells Armen that he is ready for the freeway.

"The freeway? Don't you think it's a little too soon for that, *Papik*?"

"You must trust me. You are ready." He puts down the Armenian Daily. "The feta."

The dining area blends into the living room, where Luisa is sitting on the couch, folding the laundry. Armen glances at her as he passes Sarkis the plate of cheese, the knife balancing precariously on top. Sarkis catches the boy's expression and laughs.

"Your mother will not help you. Tomorrow, we will try." He takes out a few scraps of pita bread left in the plastic bag and bites into one, then nicks off a piece of feta and points it at Armen. It crumbles between his pinched fingers. "Eat," he says. He pushes the bag towards the boy, plastic smearing the crumbs into the red paper tablecloth. "You need to eat more."

"Mom, I really don't want to do this."

"Eat, boy. So skinny. Like you can break."

"Mom."

Luisa puts down the shirt flat on top of the coffee table, straightening out the crinkles. Though his daughter is young, only forty, she has a wave of white that begins from the left side from which she parts her hair, like a brush stroke, a thick slab of paint coated across half the length of her scalp. Whenever she combs her fingers back through her hair, as she does now, Sarkis's heart pinches a little. She chooses not to dye it. Who do I have to impress, she told him.

"Papa, let's wait another month or so. Armen knows better than us if he's ready."

"He is ready."

"But I'm not," Armen says quietly, picking his nails. Q, U, Sarkis reads on his grandson's thumb and index finger, before the boy folds them into his palm.

"He is ready," Sarkis says, a little louder, bringing his hand to his throat and pressing down.

"The driving instructor can take him out in a few weeks," Luisa says, folding the sleeves of a white shirt. "They have brakes on their side, in case of trouble. It will be safer this way," Luisa continues.

"Thank you, Mom!"

"The fool will only take you out once, twice! Not enough. How many hours you need with him to get the DMV paper? Six, seven? You need hundred hours more to drive freeway good. We will start tomorrow." Sarkis points at the Daily. "Do you see this?"

"What is it, Grandpa?" Armen asks, brushing his hair back from his eyes. Sarkis has asked him once already to cut it, that it's dangerous to drive like this, but the boy said that at least he can have control over something, so Sarkis doesn't ask him again.

"If you use your fresh brain to learn Armenian, then you would see."

"Papa," Luisa warns.

"*Oof*, please. I am so old and I learn English and he is young man. He can't learn Armenian?"

"I said enough, Papa."

"You are making big mistake."

"Papa."

"Armen. Armenian. It is logic, no? It is in the name."

Luisa slams her palms hard against the coffee table, and Sarkis raises his eyebrows at his daughter. Armen grins. From the corner of his eye, Sarkis watches Luisa shake her head and then tie up her hair.

"Look at this, boy." He straightens out the paper with a crack. "The country is in shit. Big shit. Look. Just a repeat of yesterday's news. You know why they repeat the news?"

"Because the news hasn't changed?"

"Because they're lazy!"

His daughter laughs. She is like her mother in this, the way she covers her mouth with one hand as she chuckles, the palm facing out, fingers curving. But Armen has the same laugh, too, and on his face, though it is just as charming, just as natural, it is profoundly dangerous.

*

The next day, Sarkis wakes the boy at six and he doesn't complain. It is still dark out and Armen turns on his headlights as they exit the garage, the block of yellow leading them towards the orange of Sunset. The streets are empty of moving cars, though on both sides, vehicles are parked closely together, serving as a chain-linked fence for the houses behind. Sarkis and his wife built their house together, he pouring the cement for the driveway, she standing on the ladder to attach the light fixtures in all of the rooms. She was taller than him and he loved her. She was better than him and he knew it. He counted his blessings. When Luisa married, Albert, an orphan, invited Sarkis and Armenouhi to live with them, so Luisa wouldn't feel the common effect of most new marriages, that desperate longing to return to life under the mother's skirt. Sarkis had appreciated his son-in-law's thoughtfulness, and they left their home happily. When five years later, Albert decided to move them to America, Sarkis complied. Armenouhi was already dead.

"We will go in and out. One exit stop only. Keep to the right lane. Same one you enter, Armen, we leave the 101 on the same one."

Armen nods and grips the steering wheel. Sarkis tugs at both of their seatbelts to make sure they are tight.

"We're almost at the green light, boy. When the arrow will show, you will make the left onto the freeway. Are you ready?"

He thinks Armen whimpers, but he is not sure, because the light has turned, and now, so have they.

"Slowly, slowly." He twists his head to see if there are any cars close by, but it is very empty, just two or three on each lane as far as he can see. "Just let this car pass, and now! Left!"

Armen jerks the car to the side without looking.

"Armen! Always check. Even at the last second! Check!"

"Sorry, *Papik*." Armen sits a little straighter. His back is not touching the seat, but his head is touching the top of the car. Sarkis lets out a breath.

"Press gas now more. A little more. Good. We are only to be here a minute, even less. Seconds. You are doing good." Sarkis turns to look behind them and is glad that he woke the boy up this early. "You are slowing down, Armen. Keep your foot on gas."

A car honks suddenly and Armen tenses. The car moves quickly beside them, and the man sticks out his middle finger.

"I know what this means! I can do it, too," Sarkis yells, but the car has already passed.

"*Papik*," Armen says, but Sarkis can't tell if this is a statement or the beginning of question, the boy's voice is so soft.

"Keep driving," he tells him.

"Thank God," he hears Armen whisper just a moment later, when the exit sign for Normandie appears.

"Yes," he says. "We are almost finished for this round. Slow down now, not too much. Yes, good. Take the right lane."

Armen flicks the signal, and Sarkis feels the car veer slightly. He grabs the wheel and rights it quickly.

"Sorry," Armen says, turning to him, with his mouth open, breath smelling like something damp.

"Look straight, Armen."

When they get back on the street, he claps the boy on the knee.

"Okay, now take right again, and we will enter the freeway. This time, we go two exits."

Armen doesn't reply, though Sarkis feels the car slow down again.

"The light is green, Armen. Press the gas more."

"I don't want to," Armen says, craning his head to the right. He's not looking at him. Sarkis shuts his mouth. They will not argue in the middle of the street. The first open parking spot they pass on the street, Armen takes. He turns off the engine and drapes his arms across the wheel. Sarkis thought they were doing fine. He tells the boy just that.

"I can't, *Papik*. I can't."

"But you did. And you will."

"*Papik*, please. I don't want to do this anymore. Just leave it alone."

Sarkis turns to his window and rubs it down with his wrist, though it has not fogged in the morning weather. "Armen, you are lucky to be living here. Beautiful Los Angeles. So many beaches close to you. Remember when your father would take us?" He winces as he says it; they don't talk about Albert much, but this is important. "He would make hot dogs for breakfast and the bread would be wet from the water, we would sit so close to it."

Armen doesn't respond, but he sits straighter, cracks his knuckles. Sarkis shakes his head. Even this gesture does not suit the boy. He looks like just that, a boy, a child, so helpless.

"We haven't been in so long, Armen. You can take us now," he tries more tenderly.

"I don't have to do anything." The bite in Armen's voice surprises him.

Sarkis wants to tell him to save the fight for when it matters. "Your mother loves the water, but you know how much she hates to drive the freeway."

"I'm like her then."

Sarkis thinks about this. "Don't you want to make her happy?"

Armen scrunches his face, his mustache retreating into his nose.

"I am not trying to make you feel guilty. I am saying, sometimes you run, and sometimes you drive. You must know how to do these things. Life is not easy. Life is not just walking by, looking at pretty things."

"I can take the streets to Santa Monica. She can come with me. You can come with me, too. It'll take longer, but who cares? What's the rush?"

"Armen, we are all getting older."

"Listen. I don't want to drive the freeway. I don't want to think about just how high my body is going to fly in the air if I'm not able to stop in time. I can never be fast enough, you get it? I can never be quick enough."

"Yes, you—"

"I'm not made for this."

The birds, the birds in his throat, how they flutter. Swallow, swallow, Sarkis tells himself. Breathe.

"This is not who I am," Armen says, looking away.

Sarkis wants to weep. He turns the handle in slow circles to lower his window and leans his head towards the mirror. He wants to take a look at himself, see himself for the fool he is. He leans closer and pulls a small piece of dead skin off his lower lip, quickly, like a bandaid. Immediately, he bleeds. He holds his hand to his mouth, presses down briefly, then removes it. When he looks again into his reflection, his chin is soiled. His hand is stained, too.

"I am sorry for what I have done," he tells Armen. "Let us please go home."

*

When Armen stumbles into the apartment four hours later, the cut under his eye strangely vertical, like someone either took great care with the knife or very little, in his wife-beater and not the blue shirt he left the apartment in to grab his grandfather mineral water from the 99Cent Store, Sarkis does not cry out. He just rises from his seat on the couch, takes the three steps needed to reach the boy, and envelops him in his arms, rests his cheek against the boy's chest. Armen's beating heart is the only sound in his ears for a while before Luisa comes into the room and screams.

He doesn't tell them who it was or where it happened, and they don't ask him why. In the living room, Luisa takes the hem of his undershirt and lifts it over his head, Armen's hands somehow dangling even in height. He's calm, expressionless, but when she grabs at his buckle, tries to unclasp it with her trembling fingers, he smiles and rubs one eye with his fist.

"I got it, Mom."

Sarkis sees that the boy's hands have a mark of red. He surges with pride. He thinks, at least he fought back. He moves closer to the boy and grabs one arm, brings it to his face. With his thumb, Sarkis gently touches Armen's knuckles, and the red, like he hoped, is crusty. But the skin is not raw. The bone is not bruised. Sarkis looks at the boy's bleeding nose, the cut down his cheek, the throbbing lips, and he feels a powerful need to vomit. He rushes to the bathroom, heaves nothing into the toilet, but in the attempt, there is reprieve. He rinses his mouth and returns to the living room. Luisa is standing very close to Armen, he in only his boxers now, and she is looking up at him in what Sarkis knows to be the way Armen looked at her as a child, like the creature before him knew all the answers, knew just exactly how the world worked. His jeans and undershirt are lying on a heap beside them, and Sarkis almost wants to laugh at the absurdity of the scene, as if he is catching two lovers in a moment of passion, and not a mother with her defeated son. But Luisa is whispering something to him, her voice so slight Sarkis almost doesn't hear. Even now, after all these years, words in English reach his ears a note dimmer, slightly muffled, like he can't quite fully grasp them. At this moment, he is grateful.

"Did they get you," she's asking him. "Did they get you?"

Armen's quick jerk of the head is enough, and Sarkis thinks the way Luisa exhales is like a gust of wind blanketing all in its path, blanketing everything. She slumps over, puts one hand flat across his chest. Sarkis steps closer to them, his slippers shuffling across the wooden floor. Luisa glances up, takes her son's hand and tugs him towards the bathroom. Sarkis steps aside, but the guilt moves with him. Armen leans against the towel rack as Luisa moves in front of him, puts one foot inside the tub, and reaches for the shower dial. Sarkis watches them from the hall-way. The rush of water comes faster than Luisa anticipates, and she pulls her head back, but not quick enough. She's coated with little droplets, her back, her leg, hair already damp and curling fast, and she sweeps the length of her forearm across her face to dry herself. She steps back outside, both her feet on the darkening blue mat, and puts her hands on her hips. Sarkis thinks she has never looked more proud or broken. She grabs her hair and twists it into a knot and holds it there at the top of her head for a minute, just staring at Armen staring at the ground. Some sharp sound escapes Sarkis's mouth, and Luisa seems to remember he is there, nearby, watching. She catches his eye and doesn't smile.

She drops her hand, and the knot uncoils itself onto the nape of her neck.

"Go sit down, Papa," she says, her voice stronger than he expected, closing the door behind her. Sarkis obeys. He returns to the couch and puts his hands on his knees, Luisa walking past him to the kitchen. She's back in view within seconds, holding onto a pair of scissors, holding it from the tip, the rubbery orange hoops swaying in the air. She walks back to the bedroom. Sarkis just sits there for a second, two seconds, three, and then stands up, almost runs.

Luisa's standing at the foot of the bed that was Albert's first big purchase when they arrived in Los Angeles, and she's pulling out a few dead strands from the bottom of her hair. She spins them into a ball between her palms and places it on the vanity counter before her. "Luisa," he says, wanting to step forward, but unable to, stuck at the entrance.

The water pressure increases in intensity, and both he and Luisa look towards the bathroom, turning their heads slightly toward the sound. Sarkis imagines his grandson holding his face directly into the stream.

Then Luisa is taking the kitchen scissor to her hair, snapping it off as she would chicken bones or celery stalks for dinner, quickly, her eyes tightly shut, face turned away from the sight.

At night, when everyone is in bed, in their own stages of false sleep, Sarkis thinks about what he has done to the boy. If only he loved Armenouhi less. If only he was a stronger man. If only he loved Armen differently, didn't coddle him, didn't kiss his forehead while he was sleeping, if only he let him bleed a little more before he got the rubbing alcohol, if only he raised his hands as well as his voice in threat, if only he didn't look up and smile every time he walked into the room, if only he didn't spend all his time with him, if only he gave the boy room to breathe. If only he gave the boy a chance.

*

On Mondays, Luisa and Armen wake at seven, she to get to Garnik's Bakery by eight and he for Hollywood High. Sarkis always sets the table, though he knows Luisa will grab a bite at work, sneak an éclair, or eat a piece of baklava that she made a day or two before, but which the manager still makes her put out under the glass with a little index card in front that says *taza*, fresh. Though breakfast makes him nauseous, Armen sits with Sarkis, his elbows on the table, a glass of orange juice in hand, legs crossed and moving fast. They're both quiet in the mornings, looking at each other with soft, tired eyes, then bowing their individual heads, Sarkis to his demitasse cup, Armen to his mug. Afterwards, when Armen disappears out the door and he is still left at the table with his coffee, Sarkis is filled with regret, with words he could've said, questions he could've asked, apologies, so many of them.

But Sarkis suspects Armen will miss school today. He doesn't wait to find out. He grabs his hat and wallet.

In Vanadzor, in the mornings, while Armenouhi fried this and scrambled that, he used to take walks, and then once more with her after dinner, hand-in-hand. They'd circle their neighborhood, the city center, get ice cream when the weather allowed. Sometimes they crossed the long, rickety old bridge across the lake, she following, stepping on the planks on which he stepped, her hand still in his, and he turning back every other second to check that the hand in his was not a phantom. At the bottom of this bridge was a large and leafy park through which they'd walk for miles and end up in nearby villages. Before Luisa was born, there were times when they didn't even return home, when they took off their clothes and used them as blankets, as pillows, watched the shadows play across the acacias, dug their noses deep into each other's necks. He loved the walks when they talked and talked, loved still the walks when they were silent. She died unexpectedly, in her sleep, in the middle of the night. He was dreaming as she lay dead beside him, who knows how many dreams.

Sarkis puts his hands in his pockets and hesitates at the light in front of Shakey's Pizza, thinks about where to go. He crosses the street without looking. He stops at the Water Station, next to Sunset Fashion, where he knows Luisa buys those ugly work shirts—always too small, too wide, unapologetically cheap—and asks the boys there for some water. Garbis's grandson, Hovsep, disappears behind his desk and returns with an Aquafina.

"Only the good stuff for you, *Papik jan. Oor es gnum esor?*"

Sarkis raises one finger in the air, opens the bottle, and takes a sip, then another, nods slowly as he puts the cap back on. Hovsep and the other boys never speak to him in English. They shake his hand and call him *jan,* dear. They wear crosses on their necks, not earrings, not like Armen. Sarkis can't help but like them. These are good kids. Sometimes Garbis and Toshko complain, say that at least Armen's a quiet boy, doesn't get into trouble, but they say this with a shrug, a twisted smile, and he knows that they feel proud of what they've got. Lucky, at least.

"I don't know where I am going, really. I will see where I end up. Maybe the beach."

Hovsep laughs, claps him on the back. "That's a long walk," he says. "You've got four hours to spare? What a nice life, huh?"

"What does an old man like me have to do?"

Hovsep smiles, takes the bottle from his hand, runs over and gets a new one. "Here, for your trip."

Sarkis reaches for his wallet, but Hovsep puts up a hand. "What kind of person would I be if I didn't give an old man some water?"

Sarkis tips his hat as he leaves. Next door is the 99 Cent Store, the hooligan dentist's office, Food 4 Less. He keeps walking. Yes, he will try for the beach. Why not? He will keep going until it greets him, the sudden change in air, the stillness, that shimmer that makes nearby houses tremble from a distance. From time to time, he takes note of a street name he passes or watches the drivers crawling past him in the morning traffic. He feels good about himself, feels invigorated, nostalgic. A few times he even winks at those passing by him, walks a little faster. He is in his head, not quite thinking, almost resting, curled up against his scalp, as if with a nice glass of his favorite beer, Pilsner Urquell, sipping soundlessly, steadily. Oh, when Pilsner was first introduced to Armenia. He remembers that madness, the men in white trucks parked in front of the music school, selling bottles of them in cake boxes. Not the cans he sometimes sees in stores here, but real glass bottles, stubby and brown, the kind that would break into a million pieces when it slipped from your hand. It was the only drink Armenouhi had touched, one mouthful on their wedding night, in their room, sitting against the bedframe, their shoes still on. His shirt was unbuttoned, and her bulbous gown gathered on her thighs like a shield. She made a childish face at the taste, shook her head and stuck out her tongue, and he had kissed her then.

The street is less noisy now, the cars moving faster, but it may be him simply tiring. He takes off his hat, wipes the sweat, and puts it back on. In front of a Chinese restaurant he stops, leans against the glass wall where the awning provides shade. There is little water left in his bottle, and he pours it in his palm, rubs his forehead and neck, not bothering to take his hat off. He turns around to look through the glass, puts his hand over his eyebrows, and peers. There is an old woman, older than him, with orange hair and thick-framed glasses sitting by herself and eating noodles from a paper plate. Scanning the room, he sees no one else. He checks his watch and the time surprises him. Maybe he will end up at the beach after all. He glances back at the woman to find that she is looking at him. Flustered, he waves the empty Aquafina bottle in hello. She puts down her chopsticks and sits back, tilts her head. He keeps waving. The woman takes off her glasses and waves them back at him. He laughs then, and she picks up her chopsticks to resume eating.

Sarkis feels a strange sensation wash over him as he continues on his way, like someone is telling him to pay attention, to make meaning of this moment, but he just can't. He is too old to use that part of his brain. For a brief second, though, he has this thought: that his entire life can be summed up by an encounter like this, with him waving to a stranger. But then his stomach clenches and cramps, and he thinks he needs to find some *jermuk* to calm it.

He looks at the names of the little shops he passes, the L-shaped plazas housing so many of them, trying to determine which holds the most promise. He has always hated walking into a store and leaving empty-handed, hated imagining what the shopkeepers thought of him, as another pathetic senior citizen looking for company, a place to go. When he shops with Luisa, or during these last few weeks with Armen, he feels proud, confident, raising his voice in conversation, smiling more, laughing louder as he passes families in the frozen foods aisle or young couples by the beverages.

Off Olive, he finds a liquor store that does not appear crooked. There are no red signs advertising Bud Light, and this is good enough. He frowns when he looks at the price of the large bottle of Perrier, two-ninety-nine. That's two dollars more than what it costs at the 99Cent Store, he tells the clerk when he goes to the register.

"But this ain't the 99Cent Store."

"It is the same bottle."

"But in a different store."

"Young man, you are not understanding me."

The clerk laughs and switches into Armenian. "*Papik jan,* do you want it or not?"

Sarkis is surprised, takes off his hat. The clerk seems to be in his thirties, long black hair tied in a ponytail that hangs low on his back. On his shirt is an electric chair. He is not sure, but Sarkis thinks the man is wearing mascara. "*Hay es?*" he finally manages.

"Yes, I am Armenian."

Sarkis raises an eyebrow. "And how did you know *I* am Armenian?"

"You seriously asking me that?"

Sarkis folds his hands across his chest. "You do not think I can be somebody else?"

The clerk laughs again, leans across the counter and plants his elbows next to the Perrier. "You sound like my father. My grandfather, too, back when he was alive. Like all of them, *Papik jan*. I'm sorry if I offended you by speaking in Armenian. You were getting confused and I just thought—"

"No, no, I am not confused."

"I don't mean you're confused now—"

"I understand everything."

"Okay, I'm sorry. Do you want this *jermuk*, I mean mineral water, or not?"

"I will take it." Sarkis takes the bottle, shrugging off the offer of the plastic bag and walks to the door. It automatically opens, and Sarkis stops, takes a step back, turns. The door comes together behind him.

"How long have you been here?" he asks the clerk.

"In America? Since I was two or three."

"No, no. Working in this store."

"Oh, for a good six years."

"No one gives you trouble?"

The clerk grins. "A few have tried to rob the place over the years, but you expect that sort of thing. Mostly boys trying to sneak a few bottles under their jackets. You know the type."

"Not my Armen."

"Sorry?"

"My boy, Armen."

"How old is he?"

"Fifteen."

"Well, that's the age, alright."

"Armen is a good boy."

"His friends then. You know the kind," and the clerk flexes his muscles, takes a few steps in an exaggerated, hulking fashion, mimics long drags of a cigarette. "The Godly type." He laughs.

Sarkis comes closer to the clerk, puts his bottle back on the counter.

"My grandson does not have friends."

"Oh, well, that sucks." The clerk scratches behind his ear. "I wasn't exactly saying it's his friends, though. Just boys that age, you know. Sorry."

Sarkis grasps the edge of the counter. A boy like Hovsep, he wants to ask this man, but he feels bile rise suddenly to this throat. He grabs the Perrier, twists it open, and the water volcanoes out, spilling over its side. Sarkis thrusts it into his mouth, drinks, swallows. He sets it down, puts his wet hand over his face, pressing into his eyes, and dragging it to his mouth.

"Are you alright?"

Sarkis shakes his head and says, "I am normal. Do you work by yourself?"

"My brother used to own the place, but he's got a family now, you understand."

"And you don't?"

"Well, I've got someone. Nothing official yet."

"But you are happy?"

"Are you like my long lost uncle or something? Checking up on me? I quit drinking a year ago, by the way."

"I am Armen's grandfather."

"Okay."

"I am going now. Goodbye."

Outside, the sun is blazing. He exits the plaza, takes a few steps, stops. He does not know where he is. He has come so far and he does not know where he is. The cars rush past him, the colors blurring, his ears hearing nothing. Sunset. He is on Sunset. He breathes. He checks his watch. Two hours have gone. How much did Hovsep say it would take him? But no, it does not matter what Hovsep says, or how he says it. It does not matter if he hit his boy or watched from the Water Station as other boys hit him. If he was younger, Sarkis would've kept going until he saw water, until he saw blood. But he is old now, and Luisa is right, he is silly and sad. Stupid, too, most of all that. What is he doing? Where is he going? The beach? There is no one at the beach. His people are home. Sarkis grabs his hat and drops it, spits, steps over it.

He sees a payphone. He has change. He calls. Armen picks up on the first ring.

"*Papik?*"

Sarkis smiles into the receiver. "You are psychic, my boy."

"*Papik,* where are you? Where did you go? Mom said she thought you'd be back soon." In his soft voice, Sarkis recognizes fear and worry, and he cannot believe that he has done this to the boy, all the pain he has caused. And not because of his love for Armenouhi, no. But because he was scared of a little marker on the boy's body, a little mustache, an earring. All this sadness for such small things.

"I am between Sunset and Olive. I need you to take me home, Armen. I am very tired."

Sarkis closes his eyes and sees Armen peeking from his room, one foot scratching the other, as his father stacks his suitcases near the doorway. Sees Luisa sitting at the dining table, sipping a cup of tea, both her hands around the mug, eyes cast into the steaming liquid. Sees himself, standing by the door, asking Albert if he needed his help. His final words to his son-in-law. And Albert's answer: no. To this, he should've listened.

"Remember what I told you," he says into the phone. "Check behind before changing lanes. Always use signals. And when—"

"I'll be there in fifteen minutes!"

"No need to rush, boy."

Sarkis sees Armenouhi twisting the lightbulbs over his head, how, when she looked down at him, the love he saw there was the light that illuminated his entire world.

"Take the streets," he tells Armen. He kisses his fingers and presses them against the receiver. "I am not going anywhere."

ANAHIT #8

There are many Jennys and Amandas and Alejandras and, yes, here in East Hollywood, also many Mariams, Marinehs, and Anahits, but Anahits don't go missing. Don't poof, vanish, gone, never to be heard from again. My name is also Anahit, and I have been here for four years and have never been lost or taken. And I came here at the right age for things to go wrong: seventeen. Just a year older than the girls having Sweet Sixteen parties here, and weddings over there. And me? I was going to this high school because my mother thought the word "magnet" meant something special. But I attract nothing and no one. I am a dime a dozen, as you all say. Seven other Anahits in my senior year, and I wasn't the tallest, the funniest, or even the ugliest. When someone called out Anahit as I scanned the cafeteria for empty seats, I never had any reason to turn around.

I went to Northridge for college like everyone else, commuted from home like everyone else, like the six other Anahits did. The seventh Anahit got away, disappeared during the commencement address Bobby Jimenez was giving. She was there and then suddenly she was not. The fairytales my mother used to read to me in Armenia would begin like this, too: there was and there was not. In the Pasadena Civic Center, there were a thousand young bodies in oversized maroon robes and two parents who flashed their cameras at a ghost when Anahit's name was called. Her last name was Semerjian. It was the loneliest light, this flash illuminating no body that mattered to her parents and everybody who was still there.

But here she is now: Anahit Semerjian standing in front of me at the Ralphs in Long Beach, paying for two small Pellegrinos and a bag of Chex-Mix with a credit card.

"Anahit," I say as she collects her bag.

She presses the brown paper against her chest and turns around to face me.

"Anahit," she says, but in a way I can't tell whether she's confirming her name or mine.

"You are bald," I say next, because I can't think of anything else. But she is bald. Cancer or fashion statement is the question I don't ask, not yet, because the cashier is scanning my items, and I must always be on guard. The average American loses approximately twenty-three dollars a year because of double-swiped items. Twenty-three dollars is a night out at the Cheesecake Factory for just cheesecake and a fancy cocktail with sugar or salt around the rim of the glass. So far I have tried nine different cheesecakes and four cocktails, because I really like mojitos. I am at Ralphs buying a box of Reese's Puffs cereal because it is delicious and a fun snack for spending all day at the pier. You can feed it to the gulls, the fish, and to yourself, and this way I don't feel selfish for leaving my mother at home and driving here all by myself to enjoy my Saturday.

"Paper or plastic," the clerk asks, taking my five without looking at me.

"Paper," I say, and wink at Anahit S. because now there are two Anahits who care about the environment standing in a Ralphs in Long Beach. We might as well be Jennys or Amandas, I think. Girls who don't have fairytales whispered in their ears because they already have happy endings written on their foreheads. But Anahit S. doesn't return my smile; she is just standing there, staring. But I have always been here and have done what I was supposed to do. "You are the one who disappeared," I say in Armenian. Her fat had disappeared, too. The only special thing about this Anahit was her size, I guess, which is more than what I can claim. Big breasts, big butt, and a big stomach that overshadowed the other parts. But she is skin and bones now, as you all say.

I look down and pat my stomach. It does not wiggle so much, but no one is putting me on the cover of a magazine.

Before we came to Los Angeles, my mother promised me that there were people picking up girls on the street, putting them in movies and making them stars. This kind of thing happened to Anahit #4 (I am speaking alphabetically): Ghaplanyan. She was the best looking of us. Just the right amount of foreign look to her—thick eyebrows, but nicely tweezed. Before winter break, there was a rumor she slept with a black man for money, and after winter break, she was pregnant, and the video was circulating around on a pornographic website.

Once I saw her sitting on the bottom stairs of the raised cafeteria level where all the Armenians ate their lunch. She was sitting with her legs spread open to make room for her belly, and she was holding her belly like it was a heavy stone, shoulders hunched forward. I could come and go from the Armenian section as I pleased (if there was room, anyway), and that day, there *was* room, but I had to walk up past her. It was a very uncomfortable feeling, and I did not look down as I walked. She was gone for three weeks after that. When she returned—because unlike Anahit Semerjian, she did return—she was paler and laughing a lot more, but with the Filipinos and Koreans, and whenever she passed me or any other Armenian, she made a sucking sound, shutting her eyes and nodding her head, as if to a music that only she could hear.

I look at the Anahit next to me, grab my paper bag, and ask, "Do you want to have lunch with me today?"

*

When I come to Long Beach with my parents, we always settle near the park area where there's shade, and also because of my mother's small bladder. The park area has the public restrooms, and my mother refuses to use the ocean for her needs like the people tanning so far away. Too hard on the feet to walk on bright sand so long only to be met with cold dark grass; it's confusing for the skin. The first year we came here, there were no doors on the restroom stalls, so you had to take a friend (or, in my case, a mother) and a towel so that together they could stand guard and protect your shame. Thankfully the next year, someone had alerted the people running the beach that doors are a civilized way to hide the things even the uncivilized do, so I could pee without waking my mother from her afternoon naps, or from her Bible, which she loved to read, though I could see she was usually just dreaming. She napped a lot. It was the ocean breeze, she said. Could put a baby to bed. Here in America, my mother has become more and more of a baby.

Today that I am by myself, or was, I planned to sit by the shore, on actual sand, and tan, as you all seem to do. I have been here four years and still I am acclimating. In one more year I will become an American citizen, and then perhaps things will come more naturally to me. Tanning is a way to spend your day when you are rich or beautiful, or carefree, which are all synonyms here in Los Angeles. But I knew someone in Yerevan who was the most beautiful girl in the country, and she had a father and no mother, which meant she had nobody, really.

I tell all this to Anahit S. as we drive—my car, because she said she walked here—and she is holding onto her grocery bag against the seatbelt and says, "I do not remember you being this weird."

"Most people do not remember me at all."

"That's very sad," she says. The Chex-Mix makes a crunch inside the brown paper bag like it is eating itself.

I peer at her. "Do not worry. I am not even the saddest person I know."

She doesn't glance in my direction, but if she did, she'd think that I was talking about her. So I say, just in case it's in her bald head, "I don't mean you." And then: "Are you sick?"

She doesn't respond, so I turn my energy to finding a parking spot. Sometimes people don't want to talk, but that just means the environment isn't right, or the time. People always have something to say and sooner or later, they will say it, and if you're lucky they will say it to you. My father says this is how you get somewhere in life: by knowing everyone's secrets. He knows all of mine already, but this has not taken him very far. The houses around the beach are a good place to look for parking because those people park in their garages, have not converted them into a studio apartment that they rent out to their friends, like the people I know and the place I live in with my mother and father, even though I am twenty-one years old and in America this means by now both my parents should have found a real place in which to live and so should've I—one far away from them.

I have my choice of houses here in Long Beach, and so I choose the yellow one with the red shutters because it looks like it's been painted a long, long time ago. Maybe the people who live here have always lived here, and perhaps this is not a bad thing, though I am sure no one sleeps on the couch and that people actually know how to clean the house and keep doing it even if life doesn't turn out the way they expected. Though I imagine the lives of the people here probably did.

"Are we going to sit here long?" Anahit S. readjusts herself, spreads her legs to put the bag between them, and I think about Anahit #4 and if this Anahit thinks about her and all the other Anahits the way I do. Like Anahit #2, for example, Badikyan, who had the unfortunate fate to resemble a duck like her surname destined, though that did not stop all the boys from buying her Hot Cheetos from the vending machine since that one lunch when she had the whole bag and her lips were on fire. Or so she kept saying, fanning herself, very, very loudly. The difference between Anahit #2 and Anahit #4, I think, was that #2 was all talk and no action, as you all say, which the boys soon found out anyway (or will have heard by now, like I have heard, that she, in fact, only dates lesbians).

But back to this one, this one who has appeared in front me like a dream. I tap Anahit S.'s knee and apologize. "I am always in my head."

She makes a little sound, like a huff, or a puff. It's very small and cute, like a child, and I think about my mother and the way she sleeps now, her snores that don't sound like snores but like little train whistles. All day when I am searching on Jobbuilder and Monster.com, I hear that train coming, and I think, where is she going? And then I think, where am I?

"You're not the only one, Anahit," she says, which makes me laugh.

"I know I am not the only Anahit," I say, so then we both laugh. And I think, when I remember this, if I will remember only one sound, only one laughter from one body, because we are both laughing alike, and we stop at the same time, like we had the same thought, and that thought made us pause and look at each other like I look at myself in the mirror every day in the morning after I wash my face. I like to roll my fingers into a fist and say: Today is a new day, Anahit, but you are the same person you were yesterday, hoping the Anahit in the mirror would shake her head and say, No, you are wrong, today you are different.

"Let us get out of the car," I say.

She nods, puts the bag on the floor, digs through it to get the Chex-Mix and reaches for the door, before I put out a hand to stop her.

"Leave the Chex-Mix, and let's get some ice cream instead." Because it's that kind of day.

*

We find a spot near the shore beside a lifeguard's post, though he or she is not there now. Probably peeing and not saving some-one's life. I tell this to Anahit S. and she has a funny thought: "They should pee in the water like everyone else here does. That way, they could be around in case someone needs saving." I tell her I had the same exact thought last year, and I wonder if me and Anahit S. are the same person but on different schedules, like she's a year behind me or ahead. I am not the kind of person who has an existential crisis, especially one near a beach, like I imagine the people who live around here must, especially the ones who visit other beaches much farther away, since this one has become immigrant heaven, as you all say. Just Armenians and Mexicans and Chinese people barbequing on their Sears grills and swimming in their black T-shirts, driving thirty and forty miles to park in front of pretty houses and sleep on cold dark grass instead of peeing in the great big ocean like real Americans.

Anahit S. is wearing dark jeans rolled to her ankles and a white T-shirt, and though I see a shadow of a bra pushing against the fabric, I think there's no need for one. She lies on her back, her head on the towel I draped horizontally on the sand. Her elbows jut out like sticks for a fire that won't keep long and I imagine her coming home to my mother and my mother embracing her the way she imagined she would her daughter after she landed her first acting job.

"You could model," I say. "You are that skinny."

"Are you trying to get out of buying me that ice cream?" She turns her head to me and smiles like we have been friends all of our lives.

"No, it was just a compliment," and I feel stupid immediately when I see the friends-forever smile turn into the high school Anahit S. smile, which I remember very well due to its frequency in my regard and also its condescension. I guess the only special thing about me then was the fact that I was fresh off the boat, as you all say, and everyone else had been here long enough to get off welfare by senior year of high school. But my mother did the best she could so that this would not to be the defining thing about me. Welfare Anahit. On Saturdays she went to downtown with the bus to find me the latest styles. Hanging on plastic hangers in front of the stores, they swayed madly when the cars drove by, like they were ready to fly the coop, as you all say. The problem was that the Armanis were Armanls, and the Guccis were Cuccis and one of the two e's in bebe looked like c's and sometimes o's, and sometimes both. Of course everyone noticed. Even if I didn't open my mouth, which I didn't that first week, everyone knew and pitied me and smiled condescendingly. The Anahit on welfare. Number 8.

"Do you live here? You said you walked here?"

"I do, about a mile. I've got roommates. Two white girls."

I nod, and bring my knees to my chest. There were no white girls in high school—only two Ukrainians—and the white girls of college never sat down next to me the first day of class for icebreakers. "What's it like? Are they like us?"

Anahit S. thinks. "Yes and no. Much sluttier," she says, then gives me a wink. "Not really. Not as slutty as you might imagine."

I nod, though I am not sure just how slutty I believe white girls to be. I have never kissed a boy but that's because I commuted to college and worked part-time in a library.

"Do you have a boyfriend?" I ask Anahit S.

Anahit S. sits up and arranges herself into a pretzel. She smiles again, this time kindly, a smile that reaches her eyes, and I notice they are green and round, like my mother's, and I wonder where she came from, and what kind of blood is in her, because I don't know what kind of blood is in me.

Anahit S. glances around, as if she is looking for the answer to my question elsewhere. I join her in the looking because I am that curious. There are a lot of fat children sitting on the sand, or lying down on their backs making sand angels or on their bellies making sandcastles, and some parents with newborns in wet diapers learning how to walk in water, their baby knees spastically kicking out and then stiffening. My mother says she can't walk more than a block anymore, but you don't need to do much walking to wipe the table after your daughter has made food for you. What she can do is read her Bible and sleep, and really well, too. She is tired, she says when I get mad. Tired of what, I say, and she says, Everything. Like that's a good excuse.

"No boyfriend, but I'm looking. I want to have a baby so bad," Anahit S. says. "Have my own family."

I am surprised by this and cannot hide my surprise. I point my index finger to a rather forgettable-looking baby, smacking her hands on the sand like she is drumming. I know it is a girl because she has on a one-piece swimsuit to cover her baby breasts. "A baby like that," I say. "But why?"

Anahit S. raises her hands like she is stretching and then stretches them toward her ankles. She is very compact looking, like you can fold her up neatly and take her anywhere. But you can't take a pregnant woman anywhere you want to, or worse, a woman with child. There is all that weight of responsibility, my mother said when I asked her why she didn't just become an actress in Yerevan like she always wanted. This was after I got a C in Drama my second and final semester of high school and she remembered that her daughter wasn't really her daughter after all, but a girl she found in a dilapidated old building on the outskirts of Yerevan, Anahit just a name in some old nun's record book, aged two, motherless, fatherless, lonely. My mother had acted her whole life but never made it, because you don't make it in places like Armenia. There are pictures of her all over our fake-house, black and white photographs of her laughing, sometimes with her mouth, sometimes with her eyes, but always with strange skinny flowers in her arms, their buds unopened, like she is carrying wood. My mother decided to stop acting with me when she realized I wouldn't make it either, not even in America, which is where you all say it happens.

Confirmation of what she was long afraid of, she said. You just don't have it in you, Anahit. My blood.

"Hey, hey, are you okay?" Anahit S. asks. "You look lost."

"My mother uses Lent as an excuse to diet," I say. "Did you know that?"

She scoots closer to me, our hips almost touching. Two Anahits sitting on the beach. One sick, one healthy. Like the start of a joke, I think. What will happen if we step into a bar? Or perhaps the big ocean, because it's closest even though right now it feels so far away?

"No, I didn't know that," she says, and her voice is soft like she is talking to a baby, and I think, maybe she will make a great mother after all.

"No wheat and dairy and meat for forty days, and then she goes shopping after church."

"That's funny," she says, but doesn't laugh.

"What's your mother like?" I ask.

"Sad," she says, looking at the baby again. "I haven't been home in a long time."

I nod, so it can help with the understanding. "Because you're sick?"

"No, because my father is," she says, standing up and rubbing the sand from the back of her knees. "Really sick. Disgusting. My mother has no idea."

I scramble to my feet, and then I stand there, staring at her face smiling kindly back at me, and it's not like looking into a mirror at all.

*

We get ice cream, she a Bugs Bunny popsicle, and I a strawberry sandwich. I offer to pay for her, and she laughs long and hard.

"We are not on a date," she says. "And you're not my mother either. I can treat myself. I treat myself well, actually. I mean, I live in fucking Long Beach, right?"

And it's not as if she's really angry when she says this. She's smiling and looking at me with her smile, and the edges of her words are not edges but curves that I follow in my mind. Still I know not to say anything. This might be the time for Anahit S. to talk and Anahit #8 to listen. So we walk a long time in silence, eating. When I'm done, I just rub my palms together to get rid of the sticky sweetness, but Anahit S. still has her popsicle stick, and she bends down and sticks it straight into the sand and so deep that you can't even see it. It goes down so easily, and I don't know what's happening, but all of a sudden I'm crying and she's taking my arm and we are walking back to my car.

I'm sitting there with my fingers curled around the wheel, breathing loudly, when I notice Anahit S. crunching on something. Her Chex-Mix. Her eyes are closed, she's leaning her head back against the rest, and she's popping the little squares in her mouth with the confidence of someone who knows they're never going to get the chance to be fat ever again. She was supposed to be the lucky one, Anahit #7, the one that came before me.

"Why don't you take a picture," she says, opening her right eye, then plopping a whole bunch of Chex-Mix into her mouth. "Get my good side."

"What's it like?" I ask before I can stop myself.

"What's what like?"

"Disappearing," I say.

She looks at me hard, her green eyes narrowing, and what a strange world we live in, when you can look into someone else's face and see what yours was supposed to be or might still be, if the timing's right.

"Easier than you think," she finally says. "The hard part is staying that way."

"You miss your mom?"

"Of course," she says, peering into her bag. "Don't you miss yours?"

"What a weird thing to ask," I say, frowning. "My mother's not dead."

"Neither's mine," she says, frowning, too. "That's not what I meant."

"What did you mean?"

"Hey, how are you going to get out of here?" she says, nodding at the red Corvette parked just inches from my headlights. Its paint job looks new, red glistening in the sun so that it looks not red at all, but like something trembling. Orange.

"Was the car there when we got here?" I ask her. "I don't remember how we parked if it was."

The Corvette suddenly lurches forward, like it might have been waiting for us to notice it before it drove off. We watch it go until it disappears into the horizon, past the main intersection.

"Do you want to come home with me?" I say, turning back to Anahit S. "We can watch a movie."

"Sure. Where do you live?"

"East Hollywood, by the elementary school."

"No kidding. Ramona? I went there."

"Well, I didn't."

"Yeah, that's right. Anahit Number Eight. The One Who Got Here A Little Late." She smiles at me when she finishes her little song. "We used to sing that whenever we passed you in the hallway."

I don't smile back. "Who was this 'we?'"

"You know what? I can't recall. I'm terrible with faces."

"And names, too, it seems."

"Some names," she says. "Some names are hard to forget."

"Anahit," I say, feeling a little dizzy.

"Yeah, like Anahit," she says. "Can't move past that, can you?"

"You can't," I say, reaching for her hand.

She takes it. "There was this teacher in Ramona, Mrs. Donovan. She made me eat soap when she caught me copying this girl's story. I was in the 2nd grade." She laughs. "You're lucky you missed all that."

"She wasn't Armenian?"

"Isn't that amazing?"

"Who would've thought?" I say, laughing, and so happy to laugh. "They're like us."

"Yeah," Anahit S. says, squeezing my hand. "Just like us."

So I drive home with only one hand, because she still is holding onto my right, but somehow it's there on the wheel, too, steadying me.

When we enter the driveway, past the main house and towards the remodeled garage in the back, my fake-house, I slow down and lower the window. Anahit S. stops talking and she's listening, too.

"My mother's home," I say when we don't hear anything. "She's asleep."

"Do you want to go somewhere else?" she asks, and I shake my head.

"No, no, she needs to wake up." I turn off the engine and put the car in park. We stay parked for a while.

"Where's your dad?"

"Works Saturdays," I tell her.

"Ah. Which one of our dear fathers doesn't?" she says, and sits up. Anahit S. stares at the door to my fake-house. The owner of the main house brought a new one from Home Depot, the nice brown ones with the glass arc that disembodies your face when you try to peer through it, but most of the outside of my home still looks like a garage. He never got permission to remodel it into a livable space and didn't want to pay any more fines, so he and his wife have to keep up appearances, which means so must everyone in my family. We don't even have a mailbox.

"I haven't been home in a long time," Anahit S. says.

"Yeah," I say because she's said this before, but then I say, "Oh," because she hadn't said it like this.

"Do you mind?" she says, and reaches to touch my face. I lean into her hand because it's nice to feel someone so close, even when they are years and lifetimes away.

She opens the passenger side-door, and I watch her take four, five, six steps toward the garage. She knocks once and I hold my breath, I straighten my back. She knocks again and I imagine my mother grumbling as she shuffles away from the couch that, during the evening, serves as her and my father's bed. From their couch cushions, I make my own bed, and I lie beside them every night, below their bodies, staring at the black frame of the convertible couch and listening to my mother snore and the train come and my father get off the train and come down to lie beside me, while still, somehow, hovering above.

The door opens.

"Can I help you?" my mother asks in Armenian.

Though I can't see her, Anahit S. is so skinny I feel as if I can—right through Anahit's body and, there, in front of me, my mother's face.

"Hello," Anahit says in English, and I hear the tremor in her voice, how unsure she is of this word. "Barev," she says then, louder, in Armenian, and I know it is for my benefit. "I am Anahit." And maybe hers, too.

"Anahit?" my mother says, and I see that tired expression turn into confusion, the slight furrow of her brows, the narrowing of the green eyes. Then from my seat I see her taking in all of Ana-hit, her round head, the sharp edges of her curves, the effortless perfection of her deteriorating body. She would be cast the star in any picture. You would want to see her face everywhere you go, in every screen, behind any door. Like a ghost, she'd be there and not there, but she would be with you, under your skin.

"I want to go home," Anahit says, and the heart thudding in my ear is both of ours. I press my forehead against the wind-shield, and I feel myself go through the glass.

My mother steps aside and opens up her arms. "Come in, my beautiful daughter," she says. "I have been waiting for you all of my life."

EULOGY FOR ROSA GARSEVANIAN

Somehow they found out who he was, tracked down where he lived and invited him to the funeral. He accepted and brought along his wife.

I.

Across the church pew from Alicia, the wife is sitting cross-legged and still. She's wearing a cheap black dress, no pantyhose, and expensive shoes—their soles, a deep velvet red. The shoes make Alicia reconsider the dress. Must be haute couture. The fabric is airy, not flimsy as she originally thought, the thin straps across the shoulders sensible. There's no AC in the church and Alicia is mildly impressed with the wife's foresight.

Alicia imagines the wife in their kitchen. The counter is made of marble, and an array of wooden spoons and ladles hang above the stove in a charming clutter. She works ambitious hours so they own an espresso maker, and it's in reaching distance of their bistro set. The wife doesn't believe in having clocks around the house, least of all the kitchen, so there aren't any; they don't even own a microwave. A fan blows. There are strawberry jellies in six small jars lined on her windowsill, and outside, August is yellow with butterflies.

Harry touches Alicia's knee with his. Stop looking, this means. Harry doesn't waste words; it's why she married him. She doesn't either. Alicia raises an eyebrow, moves away her leg. This means, watch yourself.

Alicia has always known that she's cold. When she was sixteen and returned to Yerevan with her mother, after a nine-year absence, Alicia's relatives said this to her face. At the dinner table, her Uncle Raffi reached over the huge plate of *kyofta* and tapped her chest with a mean smile, asked, "Where is your heart?" Everyone laughed and compared her to her sister. Rosa was very affectionate, they said, always kissing her aunts, fluttering around from family to family, house to house, just kissing everybody. Last time they saw Rosa, she was nine, Alicia wanted to point out. Makes a difference.

But there wasn't any excuse for Alicia to be called an ice queen during high school, a bitch in college, snob at work. There wasn't any reason for her to not want children with the man who desired this more than anything else in the world, the exception being her. She was just that, a little cold, one or two degrees less loveable than she should've been, than Rosa was. But it is Rosa who is now in that casket at the front of the church, and it is Alicia who can do whatever she wants—it is Alicia with the beating heart. And what she wants to do now most is go over there to the woman with the expensive shoes and ask her if she knows why she is here. If the man sitting beside that woman has told her just exactly why they've come. But Harry is touching his knee to hers again, reminding her, your sister is dead, dear, can you please focus?

Alicia brings her eyes towards the back of her mother's head. Her hair is a shock-white, cropped close to her ears, but it's covered now by a black scarf. Her mother has always tried to hide the fact that she has very little hair by cutting it very short. Frankly it suits her face, her high cheekbones seemingly higher now in old age, skin desperately clinging to bone.

Her mother is a graceful mourner, and she weeps quietly, shoulders shaking, head bent. She's done this before, buried a husband, two brothers; she knows how it's done, what will happen next. She will walk to the cemetery, collapse on her knees, and claw at the earth. She will rip the grass from its roots.

It was Rosa who cleaned the dirt from underneath their mother's nails after their father's funeral. She who had held their mother's hands under the running water of the garden hose before they went inside, returned their mother to the home she was now to manage alone. The water prickled, but Rosa was gentle, undeniably, thumbing the dirt away.

Rosa, the one with the touch. Rosa, the one who touches. Alicia held the garden hose.

Alicia returns her gaze to the wife now and the husband across from her. For a second, she doesn't recall her name, but Rosa must've told her—she didn't spare any details. What the husband had asked Rosa the morning after their first night together, he waking before her. "Say right away how you are doing. I can't stand it." The strength of his lovemaking: his tongue everywhere. The promise he made when they were just children, holding backpacks, popsicles, each other's hands: "I will follow you until the very end." And where they had run into each other in Los Angeles, twenty years later: Jons Supermarket, cereal aisle, he looking at family-sized brands on sale, she fixing the strap of her dress.

She must speak to the wife. Alicia almost rises, grabs the underside of the bench, almost stands, but her mother lets out a terrible noise in front of her and she swallows the desire. *Baless, baless* her mother sways, my little darling, my little darling.

The only thing more tragic for a parent than the loss of a child is the loss of the favorite one.

*

There are many ways she can do this. Her sister is buried now.

People are in line to pat her back and squeeze her shoulder, then do it all over again, for longer, with more meaning, to her mother next to her. Alicia can say something to the wife, something vague and titillating, something simple. But maybe the wife is dense, slow and sad—Rosa slept with her husband for how many years? What woman doesn't know her husband's in love with another, has been in love with another, in fact, for all of his life?

The woman and her husband are nearing now. Alicia takes in Robert's soft face, his kind eyes and curly hair. He has dimples. A man like that doesn't cheat, but Rosa could make a man crazy. Alicia remembers lying down in bed, watching her sister comb through her hair with her fingers, remembers listening to her stories, the dirty ones, the censored ones, the ones where she couldn't tell the difference.

"Turn him on his stomach, straddle his ass, and lick the length of his spine, bottom to top, then blow."

"Then what," Alicia prompts. They're thirteen, fifteen, in their shared bedroom. They've just come from school and they're alone.

"Then blow!"

"No, I mean, then what?"

"Then nothing. Lesson one: Stay classy, darling. You keep them wanting."

Alicia feels a surge of something powerful rise inside her, and Rosa laughs, falling back into her bed and kicking up her feet.

"That's it, that's it right there. Even you can tell, sister, that I'm very dangerous."

Alicia blinks away the memory. A hand grazes her arm and she jolts, realizes where she is, that her heel is sinking slowly into the wet soil. The wife gives her a sad little smile and Alicia returns it.

"My condolences," she says, and Alicia is surprised, slightly, by her lack of accent.

"Thanks," she replies, wincing at its casualness. "Thank you."

The wife keeps smiling as she moves closer. Alicia resists the urge to stiffen, but the wife only whispers something in her ear. "I know how you feel." Alicia turns her head, raises an eyebrow. The wife's smile becomes sadder now, commiserating, but she moves on to Alicia's mother and embraces her without a word. Alicia watches as the woman continues walking across the cemetery. In the sun, the wife's body becomes a silhouette, blurry and fantastical, impossible to capture. Robert clears his throat.

"Thank you for getting in touch. I would've never forgiven myself."

Alicia shrugs. She remembers him faintly as a child, chubby, the white shirt of his uniform always unbuttoned at the bottom. Rosa had kept a poem he had written her on lined paper, the back of which was scribbled with multiplication problems; she had carried it with her across the ocean. *Rosa, Rosa, my pretty flower. Rosa, Rosa, your face prettier than the prettiest garden.* She had laughed, showing it off to Alicia. Silly boy, she said. Aren't boys so silly, sister? And Alicia had nodded, meaning it, and hating her.

"It wasn't me. I think Cousin Suzy went through Rosa's address book, invited everyone." She laughs suddenly, first at the word invited, like this was a party, and then at everyone, as if he was just anybody. Robert shuffles his feet, and Alicia wants to ask him if he loves her, if he ever did, but settles on "I'll see you at the house." He nods. From the corner of her eye, she watches as he bends to kiss her mother, who doesn't recognize him, doesn't care. Alicia cares. Alicia cares about this man who meant so much to Rosa and still, somehow, never enough. And she cares too about his wife who must've said and done all the right things but was still, still, the wrong one.

*

At the house, Alicia stands in the kitchen, smoking a cigarette. People are talking, eating, their voices low and bites small. Harry has gone to get more *khorovatz* from the marketplace, and he's taking his time. Alicia stares at Robert and his wife on the loveseat with their paper plates balanced on their laps. They're speaking to each other in murmurs, from the corner of their mouths. Alicia wishes she could read lips, but she can only read coffee cups, only the destinies of loved ones, not the reality of strangers. There isn't much food on the wife's plate. Alicia tries to remember how many children she has, wonders how big she got with each pregnancy.

Rosa never had children. Too busy for that, she'd say, smiling. Too good-looking. But with hips like that, and those genes? Her relatives couldn't understand how Rosa could not want any children. Her mother pleaded, Rosa, get married, give us a child, let us be young again, but Rosa had no desire to do so, no desires, really, except those which would give her the most certain of pleasures, immediate and real. In that way, Alicia knew, her sister was not special. Many women loved food and drink, spent nights hard at pleasure, mornings refusing to leave their beds. What made Rosa special was the way she loved those around her and how those people felt themselves to be at the center of her world and on the very outskirts of it. It was a talent Alicia admired but never tried to emulate, knowing her limits. No one in the world but her sister could love so cruelly.

Three, three children, Alicia recalls, watching the wife tear a small piece of pita on her plate. Two boys and a girl. Alicia faintly remembers Rosa telling her, in a rare and exciting moment filled with the tiniest of hesitation, the girl's name, Vartanush. Oh Rosa, Alicia had said, shaking her head. How could you? But Rosa wasn't too bothered that her lover named his child in honor of her. It's a common name, she said, shrugging, don't read too much into it. I bet a million names are a variation of rose, so don't you get all high and mighty on me, sister. That was it, too, about Rosa. You always felt terrible chastising her, as if you'd take on her guilts, her sins, just by naming them.

But that impenetrable force that was always around Rosa wasn't really at all impenetrable; it wasn't strong enough to keep out the cancer. At the end, Alicia was there to bring her fresh flowers because she could not do much else. Rosa had especially liked the cold of violets, their tinged blues, their stained whites. She had an obsession with dying beautifully. And she did, surrounded by family and friends, her lipstick on, the little hair left on her head curled behind her ears.

Alicia puts out the cigarette on the sink faucet, rubs down the little ashes from the stainless steel, and then rubs her thumb and index finger together. She feels the ashes seep into her skin, the air, and vanish. Her mother has disappeared into the bedroom, and Alicia is the only Garsevanian left awake in this house and in all of the world. This knowledge emboldens her. She unties her ponytail, brushes her hair back, then ties it back up again, this time tighter and higher. She looks very stern, almost untouchable. She walks to the man and his wife, asks if the wife can help her cut the fruit, because she just doesn't trust her hands anymore. Alicia raises them in front of her as if in proof. They are shaking. Alicia laughs a bitter laugh but is irritated by her actual helplessness, something that she only tried to feign. It's like her mother telling her as a child, if you keep making that face, Alicia, it's going to stay that way. The wife passes her plate to Robert and follows Alicia into the kitchen.

She feels the wife behind her. If Alicia stops walking, the wife will bump into her back, might giggle uncomfortably, will certainly apologize. She is one of those women, Alicia now realizes. She can tell from her brown eyes, unlined but mascaraed, the lashes clumped and flecks pattering the skin below. The wife had done her best. She had hurried, she had trembled—she's not used to putting on makeup. Alicia thinks back to the wife's clothes. Maybe she was right after all about the cost of the dress. And maybe the soles of her shoes are not red, but merely dirty. Maybe both are only imitations of something better.

II.

Liyanna wonders what it would be like to be her. Not Rosa underneath her husband's body, breathing in and into his neck. Not Rosa sipping a glass of rosé for lunch as she flips through her legal files, waits for the server to bring her seared salmon. Not Rosa turning and turning at the weddings of her many friends, holding her skirt in bunches near her knees, laughing and singing and laughing. Not Rosa alive. Never Rosa alive.

Liyanna imagines what it would be like to be dead and for the world to struggle to remember you not as you were, but you at your best, in positives, in whites, and never-wrongs. How terrible it must be for the soul or spirit, whatever it is that stays long after the bodies go. Does it fight it, she wonders. Like a Roma woman with singing hands, does it carry its sins with her in a bag wherever she goes? Or does it relish this newly imagined life where it has achieved perfection only in death?

When they reach the kitchen, Liyanna stands to the side, in the hallway, while Alicia opens the refrigerator and then drops to her knees. One-by-one, Alicia takes out grapefruits, oranges and pomegranates and doesn't raise her head to look as she lines them up on the counter near the sink.

Liyanna glances back at her husband. He's sitting uncomfortably still, hands on his knees. He's trying not to make eye contact. Liyanna wonders if anyone knows who he is.

When he was around, Robert was a good father. She could say this and believe it. He had enjoyed burping Davit, patting his son's back gently as he rested his head on his shoulder, enjoyed hearing the breathless, funny sounds leave his purple-pink lips. But he loved most, she knew, stopping their children from crying. He would lightly tap the back of his fingers across their howling mouths to create an echoing effect that stunned the children into silence. He was pleased by this instinctive paternal skill, confidently waving his fingers in a "give me" motion whenever one of the children began to squirm in Liyanna's arms. It would be a lie to say she didn't feel jealous of her husband, that she—she who was made to be a mother—wasn't the first to think of something as simple as that. She never tried the tactic herself, not even when he wasn't around, thinking Robert would find out somehow and tease her about it. She never wanted to have a reason to dislike him.

Alicia shuts the refrigerator door and, with a grunt, rises from her knees. She grabs a knife from the drawer, throws it in a large bowl and balances a plate over it; she hands it all to Liyanna.

"The pomegranates give me the most trouble," Alicia says. "Would you mind?"

"Of course not. I'm a bit of an expert, actually. My little one can't get enough of them."

And it's true, Vartanush loves it, the crackling burst of berries in her mouth, the juices staining her lips an adult-red. She's at that age now where she thinks everything in the world belongs to her, or will, if she cries loud enough. And Liyanna can't help it. She does her best to meet the needs of her five-year-old, her only baby girl.

There was a time when she thought that would change, that she and Robert would have another child, if only to make the house an even number, if only to make it fair. She had imagined boys vs. girls games of volleyball at the beach, all six dining room chairs filled up. But that was before.

Alicia tilts her head slightly and asks Liyanna if she'd like to work on the fruits outside on the balcony with her.

"It'll be a lot more roomy there, and we could sit. I don't know about you, but I hate standing."

"I'd like that."

Outside, there are two black plastic chairs folded in the corner, leaning against the railing. Alicia puts down the bowl of fruits on the ground and dusts the pleather back of the chairs with her hand. She opens the chairs and dusts the pleather seats, too, smiling sheepishly in offering. The seats have tears in them with brown foamy material poking through. Liyanna grew up sitting on worse, but as she takes a seat, she is surprised by how comfortable it is. She wonders if the old chairs in her family's house back in Gyumri—before Robert came, married her, and took her away—were just as pleasant.

They sit working in silence. Liyanna cuts around the top of the pomegranates to remove their lids and throws the caps in the plastic bag Alicia gives her for the hollowed pith and that she wears now around her ankles like underwear. Liyanna slices deeply into the tough skins of the pomegranates, prying them open into five sections so that in her hands they resemble starfish.

At her wedding, Liyanna had thrown a pomegranate onto the ground and watched it break into a thousand little pieces, as was the tradition in their *gyugh*. The seeds scattered and scuttled towards all the corners of her husband's home—her home now, too, she had to accept—so that for weeks afterward, Liyanna would find them hidden underneath their bed, underneath the rugs, on the soles of her slippers. By the time the last seed was uncovered, she had learned that she was pregnant with Davit, and they had left the country shortly after. His child would grow up an American, Robert had said. Enough of their devastated little town and their backwards people. And back then, Liyanna had agreed with him about everything.

"My parents used to spend a lot of time here, you know," Alicia says. "Just sitting. I doubt Ma comes out anymore."

Liyanna gazes up at the sister of her husband's dead lover, then looks out onto the street below them. The afternoon heat rises from the pavement, painting the neighborhood in surreal, sparkling colors. Cars are tucked away safely inside garages and lawns appear an immaculate green. Flowered curtains decorate open windows. The houses seem small, probably with one or two bedrooms each, the kind of place couples move into after their children move out, the kind of place she had imagined for them, one day.

But now all Liyanna does is turn her head back and look. There's her country behind the mountain, her mother waving her tired hand, the neighbor's son who wanted her so much he'd touch her knees while she lay sleeping in the grapevines; there are grandmothers dusting dirt roads in mourning dresses, men sipping coffee from dainty cups, leaning against the walls of homes they have built themselves.

She knows nothing has changed in her meaningless city, only her, but that is more than enough, it is everything. She wants to tell her husband this, that her country is full of people and places he has taken from her. But he wouldn't understand. When the sun shone on him, Liyanna had believed the sun shone everywhere.

*

"My sister loved everyone she met."

Liyanna glances at Alicia. "Yes," she says, clearing her throat. "Of course."

"Yes, yes. That's true. She had a big heart, fucking huge," Alicia laughs.

Liyanna cringes, but nods anyway, considering her options, her words. She settles on "I am sorry for your loss" because it is not a special thing to say. She puts down the bowl beside her feet and removes the bag from around her ankles, ties it, and puts it aside.

"Guess that's why people liked her so much, you know? Rule of reciprocity or whatnot."

Liyanna nods again, decides there is nothing she can tell this woman that Alicia doesn't know herself. She crosses her legs, pulling down her dress, and then crosses her arms over them. If she wants to talk, let her talk.

"She gave and she took and she was good at both."

"Yes." Liyanna tries not to narrow her eyes.

Alicia leans forward and rests both hands on her knees. "You said you know how I feel."

Liyanna's almost amused. "I sympathize, of course. Or empathize? What's the difference? Some of us are good people."

"I had hoped—"

"*You* don't know how *I* feel. I haven't seen my family in years. I've lost my home. Who has walked in my shoes?"

Alicia opens her mouth, but Liyanna raises a hand in warning. "No one."

The first time, Robert left for a weekend. Liyanna can't remember what she did those two days, what Davit and Gevork ate, how she managed to wake up in the morning, turn over in her bed, find no one there to lick the skin of her pillow-wrinkled and pretty face. How did she breathe that night, all alone, hands over her growing belly, with no one to take in what she put out? Did she drink her coffee black in the morning, forgetting the cream and sugar? Where did she hide the spoons?

He came home, happy, and Liyanna was too with him there, beside her. There was no need to push, to worry, she knew. She wasn't stupid. She understood men's desire, the urge to sleep with a woman, any woman, really, other than their own. And frankly, she was glad he had lasted this long. Proud, too, of herself, and her beauty, that which had kept him safely home, in her arms, for six years. She could forgive this, a woman now and then. Her father had been the same way, and what were her parents if not happy? She had had a great childhood. Her children would have a great childhood.

Liyanna wonders about her, not the woman buried in the ground now, but her sister, this pathetic creature in front of her.

"You don't have any children?" she asks, surprising herself and blushing. It's not in her nature to be rude, but human nature is only a series of disappointments anyway.

Alicia raises an eyebrow and leans back in her seat. "No, no, I don't."

"Do you think you ever will?"

Liyanna doesn't know why she's asking this, why she cares, because she really doesn't, but there is a need to press on and to dig, to return the favor, so she does.

"Just never saw myself as a mother, that's all."

"And neither did your sister?"

It's quiet now, and Liyanna turns away to look up at the sky and the clouds above her. They take on funny shapes, and she squints to see farm animals, flowers, the faces of loved ones. She closes her eyes when her head hurts and the work gets too exhausting.

"I'm going to go inside. Can I help you with anything else?" Liyanna asks, bending to pick up the bowl of pomegranate seeds from the ground. Alicia's smile is wide, but closed-lipped, her eyes sinking into her cheeks like a caricature.

"No, no, thank you for the trouble."

"Not a problem."

"Sorry to steal you away from your husband."

*

The car ride back home is pleasant and quiet, but no more than usual. Liyanna is concerned about Robert driving at night. She suspects he needs glasses, but she knows him well enough to know that he'd disagree, so now and then she'll say "next exit" or "almost home, good," and "woah there, cowboy." And she knows that he won't get mad, won't get frustrated, because she has just gone to his lover's funeral and he has no damn right.

The freeway is dazzling. She had forgotten that not all streets in the world do this, blind her this way. Cars move so fast they appear not to move at all, and she'd believe that, too, that the whole city had gone still, if the hum of a thousand spinning wheels didn't drown out her own beating heart. Things are real only when there is no evidence to the contrary. She will teach this to her children when she gets home. She will rouse them from bed and she will say, my babies, listen: you are loved, you are loved.

They've been on the road for thirty minutes when she feels the urge to grab the wheel from his hands, swerve severely to the right and kill them both. She doesn't because that's what she does—she doesn't. She does not.

She has never heard Rosa's voice and now she never will—it's almost a pity. She imagines it is not breathy, or husky, that it does not slither, that words don't slip from her mouth, wet and easy. But now she hears a sound in her ear, low and distant, and she knows, without a doubt, that it's her.

Those who can do, do, the voice whispers. Those who can't, teach.

Liyanna had learned in community college what a cliché is. Truths, her ESL teacher had said long ago, clichés are truths, and nobody ever wants to hear the damn truth. Liyanna had rolled her eyes then and she will roll them now. Those who teach, Rosa, she thinks very hard, tries to send out it into the universe, those who teach are those who matter, and those who touch other women's husbands die young and beautiful, but they still die, Rosa.

But that is who her husband had wanted, a woman as hurtful as a man, whose ovaries punished her for her neglect. An American, he had said. My son would grow up to be an American. So this is why they had come. This is why she had left everything and everyone.

"She looked nice. They didn't put too much on her. She looked—" She glances at him and of course, his hold on the wheel tightens, his jaw clenches. She hates him for being a cliché. No, there is no truth here, not in all of their years. Is he imagining her right now, she wonders. That the seams running across the leather of the steering wheel are the seams that ran down the sides of one of her dresses? Did he hold onto her waist as he undid her zipper? Did they fuck in her house?

Liyanna had always loved it when Robert undressed her. Her wedding night, he took off her slip, her panties, and it was he who had trembled. It had been months since he did so last. Had it been months? It had been years.

"Nice. She looked nice."

"Liyanna," he says, closing his eyes but leaving his mouth parted, slightly, as if filling his mouth with her, or letting all of her go.

It had been days since he had called her name. That terrible phone call had ripped it from his mouth a week ago, and he had no taste to speak it ever again. But Liyanna needs him to scream her name once more because she can't, won't, do it herself. Though that's all she wants now, to cry her own name, Liyanna. This is me, this is me, Liyanna. You did this to me.

But she is not the victim in this because she is not the one who is dead. There is comfort in that, if nothing else, and Liyanna will take it and she will give it and she too will be good at both, if not better.

"Watch the road, Robert," she says, sitting up in her passenger seat. "Want to kill us, too?"

III.

He dreams her face a million times. He wants her to stay in his head, flickering always behind his lids, forever, because she will be dead for that long and so will he.

Yes, he wants to turn to his wife and say, yes.

But dead women don't live for pain like those alive do; he knows that now, driving home with Liyanna beside him, her window down, hair sticking to her lips. Rosa wouldn't want him to

suffer. Some women loved their men happy, not sad and broken. Rosa hated misery, the way it drained people of their color.
What's the point, she had asked him once over drinks, legs between his at the bar. Shit happens, you get over it. You're going to
get over it eventually, so why prolong it? There are better things
to do, she said. And then she had winked in that over-the-top
manner he fucking loved. God, those eyes sang, her whole body
sang, and he'd move his hands over her, pulling at her strings,
making sure she'd never stop.

But he failed, she died, and now he has nothing. Only his children, and they remind him not of their mother, but of the woman he wished actually was. And this is why he is a terrible person,
because he had loved someone so much and wanted to make a
gift to her of everything.

When they pull up to the driveway, his wife tells him to wash
his hands before he walks inside the house and this he cannot
bring himself to do. He does not want to bring death into his
home, near his children, but if he washes his hands, he washes
himself of her, the last of her. You must, Liyanna says, pulling
out a water bottle from her bag and rinsing her hands. Here, she
says, throwing it. You must. She slams the door behind her.

It is nighttime. The Evian glows strangely in Robert's hand
and he stands on the steps of his home, thinking. All his life he's
had one constant. His existence, he knew, was tied to Rosa's, and
so he followed that rope to here, and now what does he know?
That it's one thing to lose the woman you love, another to leave
the woman who loves you? His sons are old enough now to recognize unhappiness in their parents, and his daughter, little Vartanush, he knows he can never look at her face for fear the wrong
name would arise from his lips.

Robert wishes the bottle in his hand was not a bottle but a gun
and that his wife had given it to him with equal confidence that
he'd do the right thing.

He takes a walk. This is the only thing afforded to a man
who's arrived at the end of the road and learned that all paths
are wrong.

The suburban streets are wider than ever. He floats, no longer a man, but not a ghost either, not enough courage to be a ghost. He was careful all those years not to let Liyanna know, and now she knows the worst thing of all: that his lover didn't love him enough to stay. The first time Rosa left him, she was nine, and because she was nine, it didn't matter. They were just children. It was kisses on the nose, holding hands under tables. It was bad poems. It didn't count. It was girls in bright dresses with hands on their hips, dirty boys on knees, pleading. It was just a game.

When Robert comes home crying after his last day in school with Rosa, his mother tells him this, that there will be others. It takes him years to believe her and he does when he sees Liyanna, a young teacher standing outside the school with her children, waiting for the parents to arrive and take them from her. A long purple skirt and a white blouse, black hair in a long braid over one breast. Of course he remembers. But when he saw Rosa at Jons Supermarket, he knew with the kind of instinct one only has as a child that he never loved Liyanna the way he loved Rosa, the way he could love her still.

And in this, is he not a selfless man? Did he not gift to a woman all that he had and not demand anything in return? He wanted her, all of her, but she never gave him this, she never asked him to leave his wife, and he never asked her why.

*

He had known she was sick. Though she did her best to deceive him, the body does not lie. The last time they had met, her hair was beginning to fall, and when he had placed his hands between her thighs, she pushed him away, embarrassed. I'm a fucking child, she laughed and pulled down her skirt, covering her thinning hips. I don't want to talk about it, she said without looking at him when he opened his mouth. You can go.

They would meet in her apartment; sometimes he'd stay for a weekend, sometimes a week, whatever she wanted. Less at the end, then none at all, not again for months, not again for ever. Most of the time they ordered in. When he teased her for having a conscience, for not wanting word to reach his wife, she pointed a finger at him and scoffed. You stupid boy, I'm doing this for you. I couldn't care less. He always wondered about that, just how much Rosa could care, about him or anybody else. He was attracted to it, too, immensely, this strong sense of indifference, out of a foolish desire to be the one who proved her wrong. That you do have a heart, Rosa, and that you do have mine.

As children, she only kissed him on the cheek, little ones, fast and magical, and he'd never be too sure as to what happened. He only knew, even then, that he wanted more. When he married Liyanna, she gave all of herself to him, everything she was. And it was enough. With Liyanna, it was enough. But it shouldn't have been. It shouldn't ever be.

Robert loved his wife like he loved himself. He could look at her and see himself and, yes, he was happy with what he saw, proud too. They were good people, good for one another, sensitive and attractive, evenly matched. But he loved Rosa the way a man needs to love. He loved her more than she loved him. He loved her because it felt wrong not to, because it hurt to pretend otherwise. He loved her because someone had to and it had to be him. To explain it, for it to make sense, that was not love. A sensible man does not know love, only the fool, and that's what his wife had called him when she found out. A fool.

But Liyanna didn't ask him how long it was going on, so he didn't have to tell her forever. She heard him cry on the phone, heard him call Rosa's name, then her own, and she had understood. She went over and brought him tissues. Clean your face, she said. And lower your voice, the children. Robert was surprised by her reaction, confused, too. Was that it? Did he even have to say anything? He was angry at himself for his straying thoughts, but angrier at his wife for making this moment about her.

They slept in the same bed that night, and all the other nights. It wasn't as uncomfortable as he feared. She couldn't hate him because he was in mourning, and he could never hate her because he never loved her enough. The next day, it was Liyanna who brought it up over breakfast. The kids were there, or they might as well have been. Conversation was polite. She asked, When's the funeral? He replied, A week. She asked, Should I come along? She answered, I should come along.

It would be a lie to say he started to see his wife in a new light, darker, perhaps more dangerous and exciting. She was still Liyanna. Liyanna was a woman hurt who wanted to share the burden. She was not Rosa who had cancer and didn't want anyone to know.

Just to do something, Robert checks the time on his phone, then turns it off completely. He crosses the street without looking. He knows there's a liquor store somewhere around here. He was drunk and happy last time he was there, with Rosa rolling her eyes and smiling, pushing him toward the water. Sober up before you get home, she scolded. He said, This isn't the alcohol talking, I love you. I know, she replied and grabbed two bottles. We'll just take these.

The day they ran into each other at the market, they made plans for dinner, to catch up. Tell me about your family, she said over cream soup. She sipped from the spoon daintily, no noise, no tiny splashes. He watched, as if mesmerized by the blue flame of her dress. Sitting in front of her, it was like he was a child, his legs not touching the floor, his legs swinging. And yourself, he had asked. You sure you have the time, she questioned him, pointing the spoon at him playfully. I've lived a whole lot of life, Robert *jan*.

Robert put down his fork and leaned forward. All the time in the world, he said and believed it.

After dinner, Rosa asked if he'd like to join her for a stroll. No one walks here, she said. I feel like it's just me in the universe, and then she threw her head back and laughed, really laughed, deep and amazing. Sound awfully narcissistic, don't I, Robert dear? God, I'll never learn. And she walked on ahead of him, turning back once, as if to say, Well? He kept quiet. Are you coming, she asked, frowning.

Yes, yes, forever, yes.

*

Robert walks ten minutes, twenty, an hour, it does not matter. He will spend his whole life walking, trying to remember, each step heavy and purposeful. He will grow old, his children strong, but he will wander the streets of this neighborhood, he will turn all of its corners, and he will not be any closer to what he has lost. Like Rosa, his heart is buried here. Here, he gave up what was steady and true for a woman who was forever leaving him but never for good, never for long. He will roam the streets of Los Angeles, follow her footprints, the smell of perfume behind one ear, the dance of her skirt, he'll be quickening his steps, reaching for her, his heart beating louder and louder, but Rosa Garsevanian will always be too fast, too clever, far too beautiful, too much, much too alive for him.

IN EVERYTHING I SEE YOUR HAND

You know those stories about old married couples, how when one dies, the other quickly follows? This story is like that, except the dying in this are brothers, and there's three of them. The first one was my godfather, the second I didn't know very well, and the third, the youngest and fattest of them all, took me to dinner once with his family, made me sit down right next to him and kept pouring us wine until one of us started to cry—him. I have a picture of this. His wife had taken it so I'd remember my time visiting them in Las Vegas. In it, my pink bra straps show from under my top and he's covering his face with both hands.

*

I'm thirteen and one month away from graduating middle school and starting Marshall, the same high school my brother went to. He won't be going to college next year because he didn't apply to any, not even CSUN, the place everyone gets into if they got a working credit card for the application fee. But nothing comes between me and my schoolwork, not my father's death, not anything. I'm going to get out of this place and be famous doing something meaningful. I'll be a diplomat, I'll start a chain of orphanages, run for governor, invent something useful, like a car that stops when you want it to, just like that, close your eyes, say stop, and you're still alive. I hate Los Angeles. I hate Little Armenia. When I buy cookies from the local bakery, I agonize over what language to speak with the cashier. I lied in fifth grade when

I drew my block for a city-wide art competition. There are no old men playing chess outside their doorsteps, no women drinking *surj* on their balconies, watching the sunset, no children jumping rope outside, balls being thrown in the air. There is nothing beautiful about my neighborhood.

*

I got my first B in English class today. We were supposed to write an essay on *1984* using the Schaffer method, but I did it my way. Mr. Roberts agreed it was a great essay, but he still gave me the B because I "didn't follow directions." Clearly Mr. Roberts didn't read *1984* as closely as I did. People follow the rules, read speed limits, turn right when they're supposed to, but they still get into accidents. Everyone's blind in Los Angeles. Or deaf. My brother pretends he doesn't hear when our mom cries putting the dirty clothes into the washer. She pretends she doesn't see the scar above his eye as he leans over to kiss her goodnight. But I'm no actress, not the way they are. I have a bigger part to play than a dead man's daughter. This is why the B is a problem. I'm supposed to be valedictorian. I'm supposed to stand in front of my school in four weeks and give them a speech on what I've learned these past three years, so the people sitting in the audience can learn from me that they could do anything, be anyone, if they work hard for it—that there's nothing stopping them. But if Mr. Roberts gives me a B in the class, then something will.

*

Not long ago, I was friends with this girl Mariah. We kept a diary together, writing things down for one another though we could've just as well said them. But it was nice, we agreed, to see our lives on the page and feel a lot more important than we actually were. I made sure I had it on Fridays so I could keep it during the weekend, when chances were greater that something interesting might happen to me. A month after my dad died, she wrote *I*

HAD SEX, just like that, like nothing else mattered, and I stared at those three words all weekend, squinting at her purple cursive. Next Monday in homeroom, I turned in my seat, looked Mariah straight in the face, and handed her the diary. I said "Goodbye." And it's like she understood. She didn't even open it up, turn to the last page, didn't even look for an explanation.

*

When I was ten, the summer before middle school, I returned to Armenia with my mother. My father sent me back as a present for winning the art competition, and I told him I would've much preferred a pony, like the other Americans. He said, Don't worry, kid. There are plenty of donkeys where you're going. This was my first visit since leaving the country at age four. As my mother and I stepped onto the arrivals lobby after the sixteen hour flight, I heard a wrenching noise, like that of an animal dying, or being born. An old man with a long white beard rushed toward us, his arms outstretched in front of him, a zombie of sorts, but much more alive, in tears and smiling. The Martirosyan brothers were always a bunch of criers.

*

I don't know what Mariah got on her *1984* paper, but I want to. Like me, she's had straight As since 6th grade. It's why we were friends. We wanted the same things. I know it's between us for Valedictorian, but my level of Math is higher than hers. All grades being equal, the title is mine because I have had to deal with harder subjects this year. But if she gets an A in English, and I don't, well, I know most people only care about the bottom line. Numbers are what's important. There's a big difference between a 4.00 GPA and 3.98. Even Pre-Algebra-Mariah can figure that out. She sits on the other side of the room during English, so I couldn't peek at her paper when Mr. Roberts returned our *1984* essays to us, and I wasn't thinking quickly enough to just check out her expression. Sometimes, even the best of us are slow to react.

*

I'm sitting on the steps of the school's main entrance when my brother drives up. Harut doesn't work on Fridays, so he picks me up because he knows how much I hate the bus and everyone on it. You're late, I say, opening the door. I'm here, aren't I, he shoots back. Put on your seatbelt, I tell him as I click in mine. He rolls his eyes and starts driving. Harut's car is always a mess, and when I turn to put my water bottle into the cupholder, I see millions of cigarette stubs tightly packed and solid in its place. I groan. What, he asks, raising his eyebrow. That, I point. I thought you said you were done smoking? Sorry, Mom, he laughs, and starts digging through the hoard with his right hand. What are you doing, I ask. Be careful. Aha, he shouts, pulling out what seems to be an unused cigarette. I knew I had one in there. You're so stupid, I frown and turn away. Jesus, you're in a bad mood, he says. What's wrong? I cross my arms over my chest and look out the window. You wouldn't even begin to understand.

*

I think the best thing about being a girl is that you're still not a woman. My Geometry teacher, Mrs. Brandeis, has a picture of her three kids taped to her desk, next to her cup of Number 2s, and she uses them for word problems. If Anthony is six feet away from Suzy, and Suzy is nine feet from Joanne at a 90 degree angle, how far does Anthony have to walk in order to give Joanne a hug? Mrs. Brandeis has fluffy blonde hair and wears an awful shade of pink lipstick that sticks to her teeth, and she tries to rub it off with the same fingers she uses to hold the chalk. The only difficult thing about that class is taking it seriously. I got this book from the library, *Geometry for Dummies*, and it tells me everything I need to know about math, so in class I can focus my energy on my friends and teacher, learn things about them that they don't want me to know, that they don't know themselves, or think they don't. The last part's the hardest to figure out because no one ever thinks they're just pretending.

*

I don't like playing games, or sports, or making conversation. I don't like losing. I don't watch television as it takes away time from my studies. Homeroom's another waste of time. I don't wear skirts to school as they ride up my ass, and I'm not going to pick my ass in front of anyone, especially my teachers. My mother tells me to tweeze my eyebrows and I tell her, That's sacrilegious. She says, Honey, *I* am your God, and I tell her, Don't be stupid, God doesn't exist. I keep my hair in a ponytail. I wash my face three times a day. I read at the 12th grade level and I know I'm ready for the SATs. I kissed a boy and didn't get it. I'm 5'8 and still growing. I'm a little fat but I don't care.

*

Harut drops me off at home and says that he's got places to be, girls to be with. I sigh and tell him, Have fun at the mall. Be home for dinner. My brother sleeps with everyone but his girlfriend. She's one of the few people I really like, so it's unfortunate that I'm related to him and have to keep my mouth shut. She's seventeen and pretty, but pretty in the way she smiles nice without her teeth showing, pretty because she hugs my mother when she comes over to visit and means it. She's skinny as a stick and she's got less breasts than I do, but I know this isn't the reason why my brother won't sleep with her. He's keeping her for marriage, but he's got needs, right, especially now? So he sleeps with the Chinese, the Mexicans, and the black girls, and comes home at a later hour every night. My mother waits up for him, sitting in the darkened living room, staring at the garage door through the window. When he walks in, he raises his arms in the air and says,

Mama! Kisses her on the cheeks, and puts his hands around her shoulders, walks her back to the bedroom. Sometimes he pops his head into my room to say goodnight, but I'm already asleep, or close to it.

*

My favorite subject in school is World History. In class, we pretend we're from other cultures and barter. During our Ancient Islam section, I was Nadia from Medina. In our Medieval England lessons, I was Rosalyn from Avignon. Mariah was a serf and didn't get a name. At the end of the chapters, we have a test, and the people who get an A get to survive whatever tragedy ends the time period. I always get an A. Sometimes, I'm the only one. Sometimes, it's not such a great feeling.

*

My godfather, Uncle Armo, was a factory worker, but he had the hands of a pianist, my mother would say. My mother's obsessed with hands, thinks that they can tell the future. She reads palms now, our neighbors' mostly, and I wonder if she ever reads her own, if it ever changes. What do permanently prunish fingers say about how long you're going to live? Or the scars from cutting all the fish for dinner? Or mine, with all the pen marks and chewed nails? My mother's a silly woman, and also very sad. My godfather, despite the tendency toward tears, was a pretty great guy. Poured me my first ouzo shot and collected Soviet memorabilia. When I stayed there in Armenia for two weeks with my mother, it was like living in a museum. My godfather took me to churches, sweet-talked priests into taking us down to the secret cellar under *Etchmiadzin*, where they stored ancient relics from Noah's Ark. The cellar was cold and damp, all stone, and it felt like we were underwater. My godfather made me touch the three horizontal crosses engraved into the wall and asked me to pray for something. The three crosses were deep and close together, their arms touching. I put my index finger in the middle one and saw it disappear. Outside when he wanted to know what I wished for, I said health and happiness for my family. My godfather died from a heart attack eleven months later. His heart was enlarged, his wife said over the phone, too big for this world. My father on the other line said nothing, just nodded very slowly, slowly, like this.

*

When I tell my mother about the B, she just waves her hand and says, C'mon, you know you're valedictorian. No one's going to take that away from you. I give her a look and she looks away, says, When are we going shopping? You'll have to look nice if you're going to be standing there in front of all those people. I remind her that we still have to wear our uniforms to the ceremony. No matter, she says. Tomorrow, you brother can drive us to Glendale. My mother doesn't drive, never learned how to because she never had a reason to leave the house, and now probably never will. My dad didn't want her to clean up after old widows, like many Armenian women did when they moved to America, so she stayed home and found reasons to clean things that didn't need to be cleaned, like the living room blinds, or the fancy wine glasses we only use for New Year's Eve. My mother washes those like six times a year. If you look at her hands, I think this is what they will say, that sometimes we cannot escape our destinies. If you believe in that sort of thing. I don't.

*

When I was ten, I promised my parents the world in song, though my dad wasn't there to hear it firsthand. It was the end-of-the-year 5th grade recital and I had two big parts: Narrator 1 and Narrator 2. The highlight of the evening, according to the video my mother took for my father who was at work, was neither of these grand performances. At the end of the show, we all came on stage with a pair of tissue-paper flowers and singing. The song went like this:

"Mother, Father, Dear. Just wait until I grow up. Whatever you want, I will get it for you then." At the end of it we all skipped to our parents and presented them our flowers. My mother cried and struggled to hold the camera still as I disentangled the rose from my wrist. I didn't know what to do with the other one, so I gave that to her, too. My mother is related to the Martirosyan brothers by marriage, though it may as well be blood.

*

For fun, I dance. Sometimes with music on, sometimes not. I spin in circles with my hands raised like a windmill in the middle of our living room. I shut my eyes to see colorful dots, try to connect them in my mind, make one big blotch that covers my eyelids. That way, when I open them, for a second or two I can see my house in different shades, yellow, blue, red. In my room there's a giant bookshelf, and my bed is right in the center, equidistant from the door and the window. That's intentional, so that if a burglar enters from either direction, I'd have a fair shot of escaping. My dad moved it exactly where I wanted it, and he didn't give me an indulgent smile like my mother did when I explained my reasons, only nodded all business-like. My dad worked as a carpenter because he was skilled with his hands. My dad was a good man. That's two things he had in common with Jesus.

*

It's hard to sleep when you know that your future is not guaranteed, but the next morning I wake up to the smell of my mother frying *pishkees*. I know what this means, that she's feeling guilty about how calmly she reacted to the news of my B. For trying to convince me of something that we both know is not true, that we get to keep what we know belongs to us. It's my favorite food. Fried dough that I like to dip into the sugar bowl. My brother's already at the table, eating the best ones—the fattest and softest pieces. I pile the skinny ones on my plate and bite the tops off each one. Relax, *kuro*, my brother says, punching me lightly on the arm. Mom, I yell at her back. She's scrubbing the pan clean in the kitchen, still in her nightgown, a green cotton dress that I used to imagine her dancing in. Harut's hitting me, I say. She doesn't reply. Harut points a *pishkee* at me and smirks. So we're going shopping today, right? I ask. Mom turns around and smiles, says, Let's eat fast. I think Macy's is having a morning sale. She wipes her hands on the sides of her gown and sits down, grabbing a fat one from Harut's plate and giving me a wink. I would've much preferred that *pishkee* instead.

*

Most of the time, people are good. Take my godfather. Great man, like I said, but sometimes he cheated on his wife. Sometimes, not most of the time. His wife's clarification but also a little bit mine. Once, when my mom and I were going out with them to dinner in Armenia, he got mad at her for what I was wearing, a black knee-length skirt and white button-up blouse. This kid looks like she's going to school, he roared. My mom shrugged and said, She probably wishes she was. My mom knows me pretty well, knew me pretty well then, too, but she only learns things after the fact; I have to spell things out for her, tell her just exactly what I want from my life. But after that, she remembers, and sometimes, this is just as good as knowing. When I was ten and in Yerevan, I had yet to tell her that I was liking it, and especially him, my godfather. He was nothing like his brother. My dad was a slow, sensible man. Not smart like me, but so quiet, he could've been, in a different life. My godfather felt important when he walked into a room, and if he could've written his life down on paper, he would've gone through books because he had lived so much of it. I wished Dad was more like him, that he took me to secret places, that he called me beautiful instead of just Ani. When my godfather died two years ago, I did not wish that it was my father instead. I never wished that. All I did in the cellar under *Etchmiadzin* was touch that middle cross and ask for my dad to be a little bit more like his brother. Just a little bit. Not all the way.

*

Money was tight in '98, so we couldn't go to my godfather's funeral in Armenia. Just went to church here, lit a few candles, cried a few tears, then returned to our lives. It shouldn't have surprised me that no one would visit us when my dad died a year later. Mom didn't have any family, only us, and the rest of Dad's was in Las Vegas, apparently too far from Los Angeles for his youngest brother. Dad and Uncle Hovo never got along well, my mom explained. It was better that he hadn't come. But she said it in that way Mrs. Brandeis does when she answers her own word problems, that Anthony had too much work to do over Spring Break to come down from college to hug either of his sisters. I knew that Uncle Hovo was mad at my father for not helping him bury their oldest brother, that Uncle Hovo would rather teach him a lesson about brotherhood and loyalty, even if Dad was already dead and gone, even if Uncle Hovo had to break his own rules in order to get this lesson across. If this was a book I was analyzing, I would tell Mr. Roberts, Here is yet an another example of human complexity, and I would tell him in a way he understands, using whatever method he's asking for. But this is not just some book. This is life and this is stupid.

*

If someone wanted to get rid of all the Armenians in the world, blowing up Glendale Galleria would be a good place to start. Any time I shop there, I see at least a hundred faces that resemble mine, only super-starved and trashy. On my way to Macy's, I pass Maritsa and Rosie, the 8th grade hos, getting their makeup done at MAC, though all the overpriced concealer in the world can't hide Maritsa's massive beak. Harut tells us that he'll meet us back in an hour and disappears. I used to want to know where he went, where he was going that was so important, that he couldn't just suck up spending some time with us, with his family, why he was never home. He works full-time now, and I'm supposed to be proud of his absence, that he's a man, taking care of his mother and sister now that his father is dead. There is so much I am supposed to be.

*

In 6th grade, I was on National TV because I was so smart, so it can happen. People are so cynical these days, think you have to be rich or pretty or a terrible person to make it in the real world. But the real world works because of people like me, people who can tell you how to make salt from separate periodic elements, which plants grow fastest in 7 Up and which in Coke, the number of speed bumps a residential street in Los Angeles needs. Producers from PBS came to my school and asked the English teachers for the names of the best. Obviously I was on the top of the list, and after a little audition of sorts, I was on TV. Me and this other kid, Louis. To this day I don't know how Louis got the job. On the show, we discussed trends in children's and YA literature. This is what happened when Jennifer Johnson asked us what our favorite books were.

Me: I'm really into Salinger right now. You know, he wrote *Catcher in the Rye?* I just finished his other book, *Franny and Zooey.* It's pretty smart.

Louis: I like *The Autobiography of The Hulk.*

*

I used to charge my mother a quarter for every thirty minutes of English lessons I'd give her after school, before Dad came home from work. I made her memorize the pledge, gave her spelling tests, and we'd act out greeting scenarios, pretend we were strangers. My mom knew enough English to shop at the Ralphs right by our house, to ask salespeople if this coupon applied to that brand of flour, but her accent was so bad, it embarrassed me to be seen with her. At school conferences, she tried to talk with my teachers about giving me more challenging work, which I really appreciated, but they had a hard time understanding her. They stood there nodding and smiling, giving me pitying looks. But I never pitied them back, not enough to tell them exactly what she was trying to say.

*

Mom and I end up at the junior's department, in the clearance section. I immediately find one that I like, a V-neck with long sleeves. Nothing fancy, but good fabric, heavy, not that thin transparent stuff that everyone could see your fat rolls in. I look at the tag and frown. I run over to the price-check scanner, but it's not marked down. My mother comes by holding up a blouse, and my frown deepens. It's sleeveless with a collar. A big one. Don't give me that face, she says. It's only nine dollars. It's nice! She points to my shirt. That's not bad either. How much is that? I say, I don't know. The scanner's not reading it. Well, let's just try it on anyway, she says. Yeah, I reply, holding it up to my chest and looking down. Maybe it's perfect. We go to the fitting room, and she sits in the corner and makes faces at the mirror while I take off my T-shirt. She purses her lips, pulls at the corners of her eyelids, puffs out her cheeks, juts out her chin. She's trying to be beautiful while I squeeze into the first shirt, her pick. I'm unable to button it, relieved. I tried, she says, shrugging, and hands me the shirt I had chosen. Now let's see how you did. Yes, I say, clapping my hands. The shirt is even tighter than the first, and I struggle to get it over my shoulders. I try to pull it back up, but it gets stuck around my nose. I yank at the fabric, but it won't come up. I pull harder and I feel my nose start to burn. And suddenly, it's like I can't breathe. Mom, I scream. I bend forward and try to wiggle myself out. Mom! Relax, I hear her voice. I try to hold still as she pushes my head toward my belly and pulls the shirt right off. Silly girl, she says, tapping my naked belly. I suck in my breath. You scared yourself, she says. I tell her, Yeah, I do that sometimes.

*

After my godfather died, my dad grew out his beard for forty days. At first, I was fascinated with the new addition to my father's face. I watched it grow eagerly, checking up on it every morning before I caught the bus to school and every night before I headed off to bed, as if it was one of those incubator baby eggs I had back in kindergarten, the ones I thought were going to hatch the very second I wasn't looking. His beard was an odd and confused gray, growing like angry weeds, in clumps and in all sorts of directions. The hair closest to his skin was white but turned tar-black at the edges, creating a thousand little shadows across his face. The break was so sudden, the hairs drained so evenly of their color, it made him appear as if he had aged overnight. When he shaved his beard on the fortieth night after his brother's death, Dad did so partly—leaving a bit on his chin like a goatee. He had gotten used to it, he said. He strutted around the house, flexing his muscles like Rambo in his wifebeater, and kept asking Mom and me if he looked good, if he looked young. When I close my eyes and try to see my father, this is what I remember most.

*

A few weeks after we buried him, my mother decided we'd visit Las Vegas and see Uncle Hovo. To mourn properly, she said, with more people than just three. Harut didn't come with us. He had work, he said. An excuse, of course, but I didn't blame him. I could never. Uncle Hovo's house was not as nice as my godfather's, or ours, but it had more people in it. My mother and I slept in the same bed, like we had done for just one night after my father's death. It hadn't been a special night, not the first, not the fortieth since his death. But sometime in the middle, sometime in the night, my mother walked into my room, pulled the covers off of me and covered my body with her own, keeping me there. I pretended to sleep, and she pretended she didn't know, but now I know the way a grown woman cries. I know the shudders of the stomach, the way it collapses on itself, the otherworldly sound that escapes the mouth. Uncle Hovo met us at the airport, but he didn't cry out like his older brother did three years before, only hugged us and smiled. I had never met him before. He was fat but not jolly, and eating with him was like eating by yourself because you made sure not to look at anything but your plate, lest he eat that too. His wife was skinny, had a slight mustache and talked real loud. They had four kids. We were there for only a week, and for the first six days, my mother and them talked about everyone but the dead. Last night there, Uncle Hovo took us out to dinner, a fancy place near a makeshift lake, nowhere near the casinos. At the restaurant you could pick out your own fish, and Uncle Hovo asked that I sit next to him. I did because I knew it would be the last time I'd see him. He ordered red wine. For the fish, he said, but it was for us. My mother didn't say anything as he kept filling my glass, as I emptied it. You're a big girl, he said. You can take your alcohol. I remembered my first ouzo shot with his older brother, how it had burned, how I thought my throat would never stop hurting. I kept drinking the wine, and Uncle Hovo joined me. He began crying in the middle of the fourth glass. It should not be me sitting here, he said, wiping his eyes with his fists. I nodded and took another sip. Anybody but me, he said. And I nodded again, raising my glass, as if in toast. Uncle Hovo killed himself a month after we came back. My mother didn't tell me how. She just said that there was something in the blood, that he was going to die anyway, that it was better this way, doing it with your own two hands.

*

We leave Macy's without buying anything, though my mother tries on a citrusy perfume sample and sprays me with it, too, gets me in the ear. It's free, she explains, and I love her a little bit more. Harut's waiting for us outside the store, leaning against the railing, next to the massage-chairs the Asians operate. He's smoking. I feel my hands harden into fists, and before I know it,

I'm walking over to him, punching him in the shoulder. What the hell, he says, looking more at my mother than me, as if she put me up to this. But I do what I want. Nobody controls me. Nothing. I grab the cigarette from his hand and put it out on the edge of the garbage can nearby. You're an odd kid, he says, shrugging. To my mom, he says, No luck? We've had more than our share, she replies, and suggests that we get ice cream. It's on me, my brother says, and starts leading the way. A lot of it is on him now. After my godfather's death, Dad got life insurance, like he knew something. But not enough time had passed for us to get the full benefit amount when he died a year later. That night, my dad was driving back home after picking up a drunk Harut from a party. If my father really knew anything about how the universe worked, he should've waited two more seconds before he made a right onto our street.

*

On Monday, during Homeroom, Mr. Demmy tells Mariah and me that the principal wants to talk to us. I look at her, and she looks back at me. We grab our backpacks and leave the room. We don't talk. We go down the stairs, and I can't tell if she's slowing down to match my pace or if I'm hurrying up to match hers. We near Room 101A. I hold onto the straps of my backpack and walk faster. My backpack's feeling heavier now, and I think about the new addition, the notebook my brother bought me at the mall, the one he surprised me with over ice cream. It's a black-and-white composition book, college-ruled. On the front page, he had written with a black sharpie, "My Valedictorian Speech." My fingers tighten around the straps, lifting my backpack higher behind me. I stop to let Mariah catch up. I close my eyes and see my father, that ugly goatee of his, my mother's hands cleaning the fish, the scar above my brother's eyebrow as he leans over to kiss me goodnight. I think about what I have learned in these past three years. I think about where to start.

NURSING

He fell in a quiet, graceful sort of way, like a diver on a famous old bridge standing still on the curved stone and letting the tourists watch, take photographs, anticipate. He fell like the arm of a clock winding ahead, just a notch, inevitability tugging him forward. He fell on his stomach. He fell flat on the dirt patch of the apartment complex. He fell between two pruned bushes of yellow roses. His mouth filled with dirt because he had time to open his mouth as he fell. He fell from the third floor window.

And he survived because he was three. Because his bones were soft. The ground was soft.

Others are not so lucky.

*

Before her husband abandoned her and left as a parting gift his parents—hostile, timeworn, in love with nothing but their own individual madnesses—Maneh Pandrumyan used to be one half of another couple. She and her sister were referred to with one name: ManehMarineh.

ManehMarineh, come set the table.

ManehMarineh, someone for you at the door.

ManehMarineh, my, my! Just how much you've grown.

They were not twins, but they were born only ten months apart. Their destiny: the same dresses, the same lackluster brown hair and quickly decaying teeth. They slid their pinky fingers around each other and promised themselves a fine sisterhood. At their youngest, when their parents still assumed they had given birth to two distinct children, they answered when the other was called. Maneh, why is there dirt on your cheek? And Marineh across the room would respond, "I fell when I was running." Who were you running away from, Marineh? And Maneh would frown and say, "I wouldn't run away from nothing."

So it went for years until that magical year when their parents understood the best present they could give Marineh for her birthday was the same present they should've given Maneh ten months before.

ManehMarineh, they sang around the homemade cake. Happy birthday to ManehMarineh. And the girls smiled at one another, put their arms around each other's shoulders, and swayed to the song that was meant for them both. When they blew out the candles, no one knew whose breath it was that reached the flame first. Did the girls tell each other what they had wished? Or did they already know what was in the heart of the other?

That evening, husband and wife held each other in a pale imitation of how ManehMarineh held ManehMarineh in the adjoining room.

Do you think anything will come between them, the woman asked the man.

The man responded, If you ask the question, all your life you will be searching for the answer.

What if it's a man?

Be quiet, wife.

What if it's not a man, but something worse?

What would be worse than a man, the man asked, amused.

Something far more complicated.

But nothing more simple in life than death. The second half of ManehMarineh died giving birth to a small, purple child the year they were both twenty, and only one was married. Even Marineh's husband, Toros, called his wife ManehMarineh. Even the priest when he had married him and the younger Hovanesyan girl. ManehMarineh, do you promise to love this man and honor this man and please this man by becoming the mother of his children? When Marineh said yes, a few steps away Maneh nodded her own agreement. So when word spread that the second half of ManehMarineh was dead, the townspeople could only shake their heads and say, "Poor ManehMarineh."

Poor ManehMarineh.

Though one sister was dead, their name lived on. The towns-people refused to change their habits, because in a place like Armenia, it was impossible to break tradition. Each time someone asked ManehMarineh how she was doing, ManehMarineh lived and died in her response. Fine. Just fine.

Yes, a fine sisterhood it was for twenty years and then that sisterhood was shattered by the arrival of a tiny, purple child—an only child. She would be an only child forever. No sister, no mother. Who does a girlchild have, really, in a place like Armenia?

Everyone believed that child was ManehMarineh's just as much as it had been—for only nine months—ManehMarineh's. How could a single father without a mother himself—an orphan, imagine that, a promising girl like ManehMarineh going for a nobody like Toros—raise a tiny, purple child—a girlchild—by himself? When ManehMarineh died, the townspeople refused to consider the connection of the child's motherlessness to her own father's motherlessness. For this was not the order of destiny they believed in. The townspeople considered this child and then considered ManehMarineh: when God takes away one mother, He will give you another. This symmetry was far more pleasant than the alternative and allowed the Armenians to find joy in their God and meaning in their ancient suffering. If God cut down their borders, then Armenians would make Armenia the whole world. And He did, and they did. After ManehMarineh's death, the townspeople encouraged the remaining sister to marry Toros, reminding her of the promise she had made in the church alongside her sister. Toros was a fine man, they said. Good enough for ManehMarineh, and therefore good enough for you, Maneh-Marineh.

When the second half of ManehMarineh was falling in love with Toros, the first half did not have to try too hard to join her sister in her profound excitement and feeling. They were sisters after all; they were Maneh and Marineh; they were two sounds in one breath; two daughters from one mother. It was only the pregnancy they could not share. ManehMarineh was vomiting every morning, and all ManehMarineh could do was rub her back. ManehMarineh was experiencing life grow from under her blouse, and all ManehMarineh could feel was life's kick in her palm. When ManehMarineh was slowly giving birth and rapidly dying, ManehMarineh was outside the hospital doors, begging to be let in.

But women in Armenia gave birth alone. No husband, no mother, no sister in the delivery room or in the lobby—no lobbies for maternity wards in Armenia. Labor was a private act, a transaction between mother and doctor and two nurses and one janitor wiping the shit from the stone floor.

ManehMarineh did not know the moment her sister passed, but she knew the moment her sister passed through her. There she was, the tiny, purple child of ManehMarineh in her arms, and the cry that escaped ManehMarineh's throat was Maneh's alone—and it was all Marineh.

Every day before work at the factory, the remaining Hovanesyan sister stopped by Toros's house, and saw to their breakfast, washed the dishes from the previous night, checked the tiny, purple child for rashes, infections, a loose tongue or swollen stomach. And as she walked home from work seven hours later, she checked in on them again. She bathed the girl and played with her, fed her—not from her own breast, though she would pinch herself at night trying to induce some kind of comfort. She cleaned the house as the girl slept, she watered the flowers in the garden, brought a few back with her inside, arranged them in tall drinking glasses. She made dinner for Toros, she sat waiting for Toros.

But ManehMarineh would find her own husband, as her younger sister once had done.

When Toros was at work and she at work, the girlchild was by herself in the house, though elderly townspeople walking

by—and in a place like Armenia, they were always walking by—
walked close to the windows so that they could put their hands
above their eyes and peer through the glass.

Ah.

She was fine.

She was breathing.

There she was, awake in her crib, reaching for something they
could not see, her little hands grabbing and grabbing at thin air.
Embracing a ghost, they would think, and then cross themselves
with pinched fingers.

The girl's sole grandparents could not bear the little girl's presence, the reminder of their daughter's complication, the loss of
two daughters at the loss of one. They could not bear the little
child the way they could not bear saying their daughters' names.
In the house where the remaining ManehMarineh lived, the man
and the woman who had once held each other so fiercely, had
held each daughter so fiercely during the harsh winters, keeping
them nestled between their bodies, their hands still outstretched
to hold one another—man and wife carrying between them the
long pregnancy of their parenthood in that one bed—withdrew
from one another and then into their respective silence. They
spent the last years of their life mute: if they could not speak both
daughters' names, they would not speak one. They would not
speak at all. They died within several weeks of one another, and
they died without a sound. They had been a healthy couple, but
a daughter's death—an error in God's order of things—could
speed up life's single-minded journey in order to remedy the flaw
in this construction.

Parent taken before child, and if that didn't happen, parent
soon after.

During one evening after work, before Toros had yet to come
home, the Hovanesyan sister still alive met the man who would
become her husband. He was lost, he said, knocking on Toros's
door, and ManehMarineh opening. He had just moved with his
parents from the capital to this small town of theirs, and they
were looking for this address, he said, pointing to a number on

a slip of paper. She looked past his shoulders and saw a brown LADA on the road and two silhouettes inside illuminated by the moon above them all.

"What's your name," she asked the stranger.

"Armen. What's yours?"

She hesitated before she answered, and she answered three syllables short.

This was how Maneh got her new name—or reclaimed her old one. She changed her last name, too, but that was to be expected. When Maneh married Armen Pandrumyan, Toros allowed himself to find a third wife. When Armen decided to make his fortune in America, Maneh Pandrumyan could only follow.

The child by now had a name—Soorpik—and Soorpik was seven when her aunt-mother embraced her one last time and promised to be reunited in the near future.

*

What happened then was life.

*

Forty-eight she was, Maneh Pandrumyan, when her husband left her, and forty-nine when her sister's daughter arrived on American shores, lugging behind three mean-faced girls and a felon of a husband, kicked out of four countries and already a criminal in this one. They were all criminals, in fact, even the children. Illegal immigrants, and how Maneh threw her arms around each one! How she kissed their cheeks and their hands when they knocked on her door one afternoon after she had wiped her father-in-law clean and moved his wife to the daybed by the window so that she could not reach her husband with her filth-stained fists.

There were two bedrooms in the apartment, and when the Pandrumyans moved in the summer of 1990, it was decided that Armen's parents would get the master, and he and Maneh— along with their son, two-year old Gevork—would get the smaller room. Before Maneh knew it, Gevork had outgrown his crib and was sleeping on a pull-out sofa in the living room. Of course Maneh felt guilty, but what could she do? Have a growing son sleep next to his father?

Gevork didn't complain, but he never brought his friends over to the apartment, and so Maneh wondered for years if he even had friends. Gevork didn't speak much, not to her or her husband, not to his grandparents who were equally confused by the tattoos crawling on his chest and disgusted by the softness of his hands. He came home from school on time, watched a bit of television as he completed his assignments, and then he disappeared into the night. He was always home by twelve, however, and Maneh took comfort in this fact, hearing from the other women in the building that double digits were a kindness not afforded to most of them. Maneh still worried. She couldn't picture her silent son roaming the L.A. streets with a group of other boys. He had to be by himself because he had always been. There was a logic in that order, too.

Maneh and Armen had tried for another child for only a few months after Gevork's birth, but it was quickly apparent to Maneh that her body was depleted of its richness. When she told her husband that the possibility of another child had disappeared, he did not ask any questions. He did not push. Armen never touched her body with suggestion again. And it's not like she would've responded anyway, she'd tell herself for many years, trying to forget the relief on his face when she told him they could not have another child. She did not particularly enjoy sex. Found it painful and embarrassing when Armen lost his erection and found it painful and embarrassing even when he didn't.

But for Maneh, to be desired was almost entirely removed from the performance of sex. She was satisfied with a look, with a lingering strangeness in the eye, a small upturned mouth. She sought it everywhere, from her husband to the postman to the clerks at the grocery stores and the young acned bagboys who helped her to the car. She was a pleasant woman, and she smiled kindly in acknowledgement of their interest, and then she shook her head almost imperceptibly in response—of course, it was perceptible to those looking. She did not entertain the idea of an affair. She did not fantasize about any man, not once in her twenty-six year marriage. Sometimes, however, she woke in the middle of the night with her insides pulsing and the distant, distant dream, as faint as a childhood memory, of an unknown and nondescript woman—Maneh did not even know how she knew it was a woman—pushing her tongue deep into her own mouth. She tried once to ask her son if he had ever kissed a girl, and he had looked at her so hatefully that she burst into tears. He patted her leg then, awkwardly, touching her jeans with only the tips of his fingers, and she had felt the softness of his hand through the denim. She felt it and was moved.

"Mom," he had said. "You lead such a miserable life."

Gevork left home when he turned eighteen, and when Armen left her five years after that, it's not like Maneh was surprised or any more hurt than she already was or had been. People had a habit of leaving her, and so it was her in-laws' constant and crippling presence in her life that she found most disconcerting. What could she do, she asked her friends in the building. Throw them out on the street? They're not your parents, they said, though they knew Maneh had no real option. A woman born in a place like Armenia was not going to abandon even those who made her life so difficult; it was a national tradition, this particular form of sacrifice. She would take care of them until they died, or until she died, and Maneh for a long time didn't know which she preferred to happen first.

When Soorpik knocked on her door, Maneh's life came into focus, and she welcomed this change and her niece's family, and finally hoped the old couple would die quickly so that the rest of them could live in this apartment as a real family should. A real happy family. But her ex-in-laws were forever dying and nowhere near death, and Maneh had to give the young family her own bedroom. She even moved the pull-out sofa from the living room into their new room so that the girls could sleep near their parents. This was the kind of woman Maneh Pandrumyan was and perhaps always had been. For the year it took for the Davityan family to get on their feet in this new country (their fifth in eleven years), Maneh Pandrumyan—who had kept both of her new names—slept on the floor in the dining room, for it was the only part of the apartment with decent carpeting.

The year the Davityans joined her was the best year of her life as Maneh Pandrumyan. The three mean-faced girls turned out to love her, sat by her feet as they sprawled on the floor to watch television, turning their heads back to smile at her during commercial breaks, their teeth spotted with chocolate, their lips with potato chips. The felon husband teased her and praised her for the quality of her meals and the strength in her arms—you could work construction with me, he'd say, winking his good eye. And Soorpik, sweet, sweet Soorpik, daughter of her dear dead sister, called her Mama the way her own son never once did. Always Mom, never Mama—that was Gevork. And never *mama jan*, a term of endearment reserved only for those you really, truly loved. But *mama jan, mama jan*, Soorpik would sing, kissing her on the cheek as she left with her husband for a night out in Los Angeles. You're the best babysitter in the world. And it never crossed Maneh's mind to remind the girl that she was her aunt now, after all this time, and would never be her mother—or anyone's mother—ever again.

Mama jan, mama jan, Soorpik would sing, and Maneh was a bird eating from her beggar's hand.

*

Maneh and her niece were sitting on their balcony with a cup of coffee on the fold-out table between them. The boy had yet to fall. Maneh was knitting, the purple needles in her hand pointed toward each other, a red hoop around one, a swelling scarf in the other. Soorpik had colored her hair again, and this time it was a shock violet, jarring on her pale, pale skin.

"I liked the brown better," Maneh said, not looking up from her knitting. The needles clinked together.

142 · naira kuzmich

"I looked like a mouse with the brown."

"You looked beautiful."

"Oh *mama jan*," Soorpik said, waving her hand in disregard and pleasure.

"Don't *mama jan* me. I know why you're here."

"And why am I here?"

"You only come by these days if you need something." Maneh put down her knitting and reached for the demitasse cup. "What is it this time?"

"Don't say that. You know I love you."

"Of course." Maneh took a sip and brushed her upper lip with her tongue. Coffee was still hot. "Why didn't you bring the girls?"

"They're in school." Soorpik balanced her own saucer on her lap and, with her back held straight, brushed her hair back from her face, smiling silver at her aunt-mother. Soorpik was too old for braces, but her teeth demanded it. Each time she pulled a tooth due to decay, the remaining teeth huddled together, crossing each other's paths.

"You've pulled the girls out of class for sillier things."

"They should have fun, my kids. Too much work can kill their spirits."

"Those kids have too much spirit, if you ask me." Maneh didn't smile at her. "Like their mother."

The Davityans had been in this country for five years—they could've been citizens now, if they weren't illegal—and they had spent the last four years disappointing Maneh Pandrumyan. Last New Years' Eve, the Davityans had dropped by Maneh's home for only an hour, didn't even want to eat her kyofta that she had slaved for two days preparing. We're too full, they said, from other visits, and still had more people to see. I'm just a stop along the chain, Maneh had said, hoping to be contradicted, but Petros had laughed his drunken laugh and picked up the keys and dangled them in front of Soorpik's overly made-up face. You'll have to drive, woman. Soorpik was quick to stand and sway, giggling as she grabbed it from his hands. Maneh found nothing funny in this exchange, and neither did the youngest girl, Azatuhi. Just seven then, but already smarter than the other two, just seven and already embarrassed of her parents, but also of her great-aunt-slash-grandmother, who brought them expensive presents even though they only saw her twice a year nowadays. Even though they lived in the same neighborhood. Even though they had used her shampoo and eaten her casseroles and slept in her bed for the first year they were in this country. When Azatuhi looked up at Maneh, she no longer smiled. Her teeth were spotless and strong. Maneh loved this girl best but did not want her pity. Maneh did not want anyone's pity.

"Nothing wrong with a little bit of spirit, you know," Soorpik said, tilting her head to look at Maneh with blue eyes. Soorpik used to wear glasses when she had just come from Sweden, and Maneh liked that look on her, made her seem like an intellectual, serious and business-minded, like Maneh imagined all the Swedes were. But within two years' time in America, Soorpik was wearing contact lenses, and not even lenses in her own eye color. And Maneh was forced to remember that the Davityan family was kicked out of sensible Sweden for good reason. "You could learn a thing or two from my kids," Soorpik was saying.

Maneh took up her needles again and bristled, swooping the yarn quickly around the frame, her hands working fast. All instinct and no purpose—that's how Maneh knitted nowadays. Who wore scarves in Los Angeles? She had knitted a million of them. If she thought about her life in the same manner, she'd just up and kill herself. So she tried hard not to think about much, not to remember, not to analyze each slight against her. But with Soorpik sitting there in front of her, staring at her with her false blue eyes, it was impossible not to rank her niece's betrayals above everyone else's. During moments like these, Maneh had thoughts like this: not only did she kill her own mother, but this girl was hell-bent on taking *her* to the grave, too. Thoughts like this: her father was smart to marry her off the moment she turned seventeen and cut his losses short. Just one loss was enough for Toros.

"I don't say that to hurt you, *mama jan*," Soorpik said, dropping her voice like she did not want anyone else to hear. They were seated on the balcony that overlooked the main street. Kingsley Drive cut through Sunset, and Maneh spent four hours a day at that intersection, baking pastries, logcakes, macaroons. She had been working at this Armenian bakery since she had arrived in America. It was afternoon, and not many cars were driving through Kingsley Drive, nor pedestrians walking home from school or work on its sidewalks. It was not as if anyone was around to hear a stranger's apology and take delight in it.

Which was why Maneh clicked her tongue, raised her eyebrows, and asked, "Just why are you whispering?"

Soorpik leaned back into her seat. This time, the cup rattled in her lap, and the coffee spilled onto the saucer, spattering lightly on her dress. "Damn it," Soorpik said, picking up the demitasse and holding it to her side as it slowly dripped onto the wooden floor. With the other hand she brought the saucer from her lap to her lips and slurped the cooling coffee.

Maneh put down her knitting and watched.

"What?"

Maneh shrugged. "I do have napkins."

"You sure you haven't used them all cleaning the shit from your in-laws' behinds?"

Maneh blinked.

"Oh God, I'm sorry. You know I didn't mean that," Soorpik said, putting both saucer and demitasse cup onto the table between them.

"No, no," Maneh said, sliding her fingers along the violet rods. "You have always said what you wanted to say. Don't apologize now, and not again, not so quickly, one after the other."

Soorpik sighed theatrically, leaning so far back into her seat that Maneh thought she was going to topple over, as if what Maneh said had knocked the breath right out of her. But Maneh knew the girl could take a beating. Maneh wasn't an idiot.

Soorpik narrowed her eyes at the coffee stain on her dress and brought the fabric high to her mouth to spit. White thighs and yellow bruises and bright red underwear. Maneh looked away. Half of Maneh's own dowry was recycled because Marineh could no longer use them where she had gone. As Soorpik began to rub the fabric together, trying to remove the stain, Maneh recalled all the times she had put on her younger sister's underwear. She had felt no closer to Marineh or to the man she was trying to seduce whilst in them. Armen did not understand the need for lingerie, and each time that first year of marriage Maneh showed him her new old panties, tugging her skirt down bashfully, he'd grimace like she was gifting him a puzzle he had no way of solving.

Soorpik brought the skirt of her dress over her knees again and let out another sigh. The girl was full of so many exaggerated sounds; Maneh wondered what sounds she made for her husband.

"I am really sorry, *mama jan*. I meant it. I'm just in an awful mood these days."

Maneh frowned, unable to help herself or her love. "What's wrong?"

"I'm having another girl."

Maneh wasn't expecting that. "You're pregnant?"

"For now."

Maneh shook her head, though she understood quite clearly. "You don't mean that."

Soorpik shrugged, and patted down her dress absentmindedly.

Maneh felt the need to stand. She walked toward the railing of the balcony and looked down the street, gripping the iron bars. The sun was behind the clouds, but it somehow reached her eyes, blurring everything. "Why don't you just push him off of you, Soorpik?"

When Soorpik didn't respond, Maneh turned her head to look at her. Soorpik caught the concern on her face and smiled. The braces in her mouth glinted. The sight of her dead sister's daughter's mouth full of silver reminded Maneh of her dead parents in the ground so far away from where she now stood. Unfair, how her ex-in-laws still had great teeth. Maneh turned back to the street, needing the distraction. Dentures, Soviet made. Could even take a bombing, Maneh thought. If she put a bomb in their mouths, they'd probably survive it, teeth intact. The dentists in

Los Angeles were all crooks. Maneh's capped teeth had to be replaced every year, and her niece's braces had cost her a fortune. Of course it was Maneh who had paid for Soorpik's procedure. The Davityans' financial situation was a rollercoaster. Sometimes there was no money, sometimes too much. Maneh did not believe construction work was that unpredictable a career, but knew better than to ask how they were able to afford the RangeRover six months after they were evicted from their Los Feliz apartment. Maneh had told them they could move back in with her, but Soorpik had scoffed at the suggestion, complaining of the "old people smell."

"Back in our day," Maneh began, pushing her face toward the sun that hid from her, "the best contraception was a firm no. No thank you." She moved her hands from the railing and brought them to her face, rubbing her eyes. So close to her nose, her hands smelled like a dampened fire, wood sizzling and sighing like a trace of sickness.

"So you were saying no to Armen all these years, were you?"

"What happened with me had nothing to do with my husband."

"Your ex-husband."

"I only had enough in me for one child."

"Like my mother," Soorpik said.

Maneh twisted her neck to glance at her, but Soorpik was staring at her lap.

"My other mother, I mean."

"Your only mother, yes. She only had enough life for you."

"At least you're still alive."

Maneh didn't respond and then thought otherwise. She turned around and pressed her back into the railing. The cold bars made her stand taller, a reminder of how to stand. "I'm not dead yet, you mean."

Soorpik tried to smile at her, and Maneh recognized the strain on the girl's face. Soorpik looked best not smiling. As they grew older, her daughters did, too. Mean-faced but handsome, they were. Their lips thinned out if they smiled long, and their nostrils flared. Maneh wondered if it was Petros, their felon-father, who had warned them against such happiness. She refused to believe they inherited it from their mother and that their mother had inherited it from her sister.

"I ain't dead yet either, old woman," Soorpik said, her mouth settling into a smirk. But still, there, the unbecoming flaring nose. "I like sex, you know. I *don't* want him off of me."

Maneh stiffened, feeling the redness rise to her cheeks. She let the heat move her. She turned to the street and tried to focus her eyes on something beautiful. With each passing year, she needed more and more breaks from her caretaking duties. She wished she smoked. Had a real reason to stand in the balcony and watch strangers become familiar, lovely.

Across from her building was another apartment complex, four stories tall and painted blue, the biggest one on their block. Full of Armenians and Mexicans and just two white elderly couples who had lived there long. The appearance of their Los Angeles neighborhood had changed over the years, but Maneh suspected the insides of their apartments hadn't. In the twenty years she had been in this country, living on this street, Maneh had seen these couples only on three separate occasions—and that third time, the two couples appeared together. They were taking a stroll around the block, taking up the entire sidewalk, walking side-by-side, as if numbers could actually mean something like strength here. If she had a cigarette, she would've thrown it at their heads, and Maneh thought of saying something to them, but then she heard her mother-in-law's grating laugh from the bedroom. Sometimes the old bat would laugh for hours at nothing in particular, and Maneh would resist the urge to stuff her mouth with soap in order to make them both feel clean. The only thing the soap would've cleaned was the old woman's teeth, and Maneh wanted them to rot. False teeth, sadly, never did.

"I said, I like sex," Soorpik repeated, and Maneh cringed at the taunting and bemused note in her niece's voice.

"Aren't you something special," Maneh said, staring at the apartment complex in front of her. Facing the street were four rows of three windows, and Maneh squinted her eyes at each one, trying to peer through. She knew which residents were Armenians and which Mexicans by the window-coverings: curtains, Armenians; vertical blinds, Mexicans. She wondered what the white people used to cover their windows (the elderly couples lived in the back of the building). Probably nothing, Maneh surmised. What could they have to hide?

"Sometimes my man is not even on top," Soorpik said. "Hell, most of the time I am."

As Maneh suspected, the curtains were drawn in the Armenian residences, but as she moved her gaze away from them, she saw a flutter from the corner of her eye. On the third floor, standing behind a crème-colored curtain and facing the glass—facing her—there appeared suddenly a little boy. Maneh didn't recognize this boy. Probably the son of a guest, she thought, smiling at him, though she knew he could not see her.

"And under me, my man is grateful. I am like his God."

Maneh tried to pay her no mind. She did not like the games of adults. She would rather watch the child playing behind the curtains. The boy was putting his hand to the glass as if trying to make invisible marks with his palms. But the weather was pleasant. Maneh knew the glass did not fog. There was no need for the boy to play there, she thought, frowning, leaning into the railing as she watched him behind the tall paneled window. She could not see the boy's knees, or anything below the pane, and was momentarily relieved. It would be almost impossible for him to fall.

"Parents these days," Maneh said, "like to let their children go wild. They think nothing will hurt them just because in this country they are free."

"What are you going on about?" Soorpik said.

Maneh turned to her. "What are *you* going on about?"

Soorpik rolled her eyes. "I'm saying it's not the sex. We just don't want another girl."

"This isn't new information," Maneh said. "I know you had an abortion before."

"Two, actually," Soorpik said, almost proudly.

When Maneh grabbed her heart, Soorpik blushed and folded her hands in her lap. "I just don't want to lie to you."

"Two girls?" Maneh whispered.

Soorpik bit her lower lip and remained silent.

"Two girls?"

"What would I do with five daughters?" Soorpik burst. "Start my own girl group?"

"You'd have someone else to take care of you when you're older. You think a boy would do that? You see my kid around?"

"I don't need anyone to take care of me when I'm older."

"Chances are one of your five would be a good daughter."

"I still have my three."

"I thought you said you didn't need anyone to take care of you?"

Soorpik narrowed her eyes. "I don't. I won't. I'm just telling you I know I have good kids."

"And you might've had more."

"Look. Just because you couldn't have more doesn't mean you have a right to judge."

"But because they were girls, Soorpik jan? That's why? Not because of money, not because of health, or anything else?"

"It's my right," Soorpik said deliberately. "I don't need a reason. This is America."

"Exactly, dear," Maneh sighed. "This is America. Girls are wanted here."

Soorpik folded her arms across her chest. "Not all girls."

"I guess not." Maneh turned back to the street. "Not yours." The boy wasn't by the window when Maneh looked, and for the terrifying second it took for her eyes to trail down to the ground floor of the complex, the small garden outlining the building, her heart beat loud in her throat and ears and the tips of her fingers holding onto the black railing.

"I didn't come here for your blessing."

Maneh let out a breath at the sight of the undisturbed flower patch. "Then why did you come?" She heard the chair screech backwards, felt the air behind her change. Soorpik had stood.

"I'm not sure. But I'm leaving now."

Maneh didn't turn around.

"I said I'm leaving."

"Then, go."

"Give me a hug."

Maneh turned around, surprised and pleased, but Soorpik was staring at her with the same hateful expression that her own boy once did. "You're angry."

"Anger's good for you," Soorpik spit. "Try it some time."

Maneh turned her back to her. "I've lived a long time, Soorpik. Twice the life you've lived. I've lived your mother's life, too."

"You've lived everyone's life, is that it? That's what makes you a good judge? You'd send me to hell, would you?"

Maneh didn't smile when the boy appeared again. "I think you've already been through that, my girl." She watched him pat his little hands on the window. He was fatter than Gevork at that age. Too skinny, her boy, never enough meat on him, but Maneh remembered that he ate everything she put before him. Where did that food go, she'd think in the evenings. Was he sick? Was he sick in another way, the way girls in this country were often sick? She would leave the small television on in the ex-in-laws' bedroom as she worked cleaning them or feeding them. She had heard a lot of movies, T.V. shows, her back turned toward the screen. She just needed the fullness in the house, someone speaking above her and under her, through her, even if the speakers spoke a strange tongue, about strange troubles she had never before considered but increasingly found threatening as she considered Soorpik's young girls. Would they protect one another when the time came? Would they come when the other was called? Or did they only think of themselves, think they were only ones in this big, bright country, this big, bright world? As a child Maneh never thought she was alone, and now, with her in-laws just a few feet away from her, almost wherever she went, she knew she never would be. It's what naming did in a place like Armenia. Carved it down in stone, if not paper. Carved it down in skin, in hers.

"*Mama jan*," Soorpik began, stepping closer to stand behind her, and Maneh felt the ghost of the girl's embrace. She shut her eyes and allowed herself the pleasure. When she opened them, her eyes made contact with the boy's. He was hitting his fists on the glass, beaming, and Maneh was about to smile at him, too, when Soopik whispered "My God," and Maneh suddenly realized it was not glass that he was hitting after all, but the thin mesh window screen.

"He's going to fall," Soorpik said softly, and then started shouting. "Get away from there!" There was no shadow of an adult in sight behind the curtains. Only the boy in front of the pale colored fabric.

Maneh recognized the pronounced dents the boy was making on the screen and felt her knees turn to water; she gripped onto the railing. Soorpik began to jump up and down in place, waving her hands. "Someone, anyone! Hey! Hey!"

"Don't," Maneh found the voice to utter. She recognized the boy's eyes latching onto Soorpik's. The reach of his smile extending. He was thinking this woman was saying hello, speaking to him. He was going to try to speak back, make contact. He wanted to play. He thought he was playing.

Soorpik stopped jumping, turned to her, and asked why. Maneh pointed, and the answer revealed itself in the slow, graceful fall of the child. The screen under him gave away, and down he went on his stomach, like he was riding his own magic carpet towards the beautiful valley below. Soorpik screamed, threw herself into the railing with her hands outstretched, like there was a chance she could reach him. Maneh unlatched her fingers from the iron and grabbed her niece's shoulders, pulled her back, her own heart nowhere near her body.

"Where's your phone? Where's your phone?" Soorpik began to rave.

Maneh blinked uncomprehendingly at Soorpik and then turned back toward the neighbor's window. There were multiple faces now, their mouths open in horror, looking down at the ground from so far above, but she could not hear their screams.

She thought there was dirt in their mouths, or perhaps it was dirt in her own ears. The only thing that made its way through to her was "phone, phone, phone."

"Your phone!"

"What are you going to do?"

Soorpik looked at her like she was an idiot, her mouth agape, something foreign in her eye. "911, what do you think I'm going to do?"

Maneh looked back across the street. A group of people were huddled around the rose bushes, and now she heard their sounds. Their voices were already hoarse, thinned out, their words dropping off like when the antennae atop her building spun too wildly with the wind, making her miss the climax to the movies she heard but did not have time or desire to watch. "Bleeding." "Where." "Moving." "Dead." "God." These were the words she heard from her neighbors, as if they had been saying it all their lives. Or perhaps this was always the way they reached her dirt-stuffed ears.

"You can't call 911," Maneh heard herself saying.

Soorpik looked at her wildly. She looked like an animal to Maneh. Her nostrils were swollen, her lips thin and long like a blade, sweat glistening on her pretty face. The most alive she had looked to Maneh, more beautiful like this than when she was laughing, giggling at her felon-husband.

"They'll ask too many questions," Maneh said slowly. She felt like she was talking to a drunk, but that was the only way she could make it clear to them both what she was realizing. "They'll want to know who you are."

"I know who I am," Soorpik screamed. "Where is the god-damn phone?"

"They'll take the child away from his parents."

"So?" Soorpik cried, pointing at the neighbor's general direction. "Let them. They should've been watching him." She ran inside the apartment and Maneh followed slowly behind. Soorpik was throwing the cushions away from the pull-out sofa, looking for the phone, and Maneh thought of how it had looked so much better in her old bedroom, with the three Davityan girls sleeping snug against each other.

"They'll take you," Maneh said gently. "You are not supposed to be here."

"What?" Soorpik said, moving on to the dining room.

"They'll take you away. They'll know you aren't supposed to be here. They'll deport you, Soorpik jan."

"No, they won't."

"I'll call. You should go."

"No one gives a damn about us. No one will come looking for you or for me."

"I'm sure someone probably called already."

"Tell me where your phone is."

Maneh reached for her shoulder. "And where is your phone?"

Soorpik stared at her.

"Go home, Soorpik jan."

"My phone." Soorpik grabbed her purse hanging from the dining room chair. "What an idiot."

Maneh watched silently as Soorpik rifled through her purse. The sounds of her niece's world colored her ears: the rattle of pills, the crinkle of tampon wrappers or old candy, keys to a car she knew Soorpik could not afford and an apartment smaller than the bedroom in which she and her family had spent the first year they were in America. Maneh could not help but turn red, for she felt red all over. She thought about Soorpik's underwear—how she wore that color with pride, even where no one could see. But no, no, Maneh thought. Soorpik wasn't fooling her.

But let it be known that Maneh Pandrumyan hadn't even smiled at the birth of her own son. She screamed and screamed her way through it, and when the doctor gave him to her, she felt the screams burrowing themselves in her throat. What she really wanted to do was release it into the child's face. It was the ghost of her sister who had done that difficult work for her. Marineh was in that hospital room with her—no rules against ghosts in Armenian hospitals. Her sister had died, but Maneh knew that a part of her lingered still in her own body. At first she thought that maybe it was the child within her, but the child was not tiny nor was he purple the way Marineh's girl had been. Gevork was born fat and full and pink, and it was only after he was born that he stopped eating. What then filled him with any sort of sustenance was Marineh's spirit, Marineh screaming her sister's cries into his little mouth.

Of course Gevork was a ghost. What else would the son of a dead woman be? Of course Gevork ate everything his mother put in front of him and did not gain a pound.

Eighteen years of life in that house where no one loved anyone else, where his own mother was only a faint reminder of her former self. ManehMarineh. People always talk about the parents' grief at losing a child. Nothing more unbearable, they lament. More unnatural. But a sister losing a sister meant losing one's own very self. Maneh was not a shell of what she used to be—she was a shell of what they once were.

Maneh would die refusing to look at herself in the mirror or any other reflective screen.

"Your life is going to be hard, Soorpik," Maneh said. She was not thinking about her son, or her life, the numerous slights against her; she was busy surviving, looking after others because it was easier than looking after herself. "Harder than it already is."

"Stop making this about me, Jesus Christ! A boy is hurt, maybe even dead. Don't you care?"

"Take your daughters and bring them home to me. You can come, too, when you're ready."

"My children are just fine, thank you. They're not falling out of windows."

"I will take care of them."

"Like you take care of that fag's parents?"

"Do not be so cruel, Soorpik jan. People are doing their best to live."

"I'm alive, goddamn it. I ain't close to dying."

"You've been dying since day one. I've been dying since that day, too. It's a long dying for some of us."

Soorpik threw her hands in the air, and Maneh noticed the

phone almost slip from her fists. "I'm not anyone's doormat. Please just get over yourself or whatever it is you're not over."

"He's got his prints all over you."

"I want a boy, too, for God's sake! I always have!"

"Nothing will change in this city, or the next, you hear? Not this country or the next. Not your sixth or your seventh. Come home to me. I won't have you on your knees or your back. You will rest your feet."

"*Mama jan,*" Soorpik sighed. "Enough." She flipped open the phone. "You've got this all wrong. Some of us are happy even when we aren't smiling. Some of us don't want to flaunt our happiness in front of those who have never known it."

Maneh shook her head. "Don't lie to yourself. You don't really mean that. And I have known happiness. I have."

"With my mother, I know. When you were a little girl. But look at me, *mama jan.* I'm a grown-ass woman, and I'm still happy. Or as close to happy as a grown woman can get."

"You're miserable," Maneh said. "You said so yourself."

"No, *mama jan,*" Soorpik said, taking a chair and sitting down. She pressed the three buttons forcefully. "You are."

"Your children need their mother," Maneh cried. "They'll take you away."

Soorpik put the phone to her ear and smiled sadly, and her lips were still daggers. They had cut through her mother's womb—of course there was no need for strong teeth, Maneh thought. She had paid so much for nothing.

"Soorpik," she tried one last time. "They will take you away."

"Then they'll have you, won't they?"

All Maneh could hear was the ambulance sirens coming, and it sounded like the crazy laugh of the old woman dying in the other room.

AZNIV PANOSYAN, IN CONTRAST

In the tape I watch now, after the children are in bed, my wife is in her '93 Camry, the nose of the Corvette that slammed into her blocking her driver-side door. The gray of the Corvette's steel frame is bloodied by its own red body and curled forward like a fist. The driver, an older white man, is standing beside the two cars in the middle of Sunset Boulevard, his hands around his mouth, shouting, "You alright? You alright?" All of Los Angeles is slowing down as they pass my wife, then speeding back up. The person taking the video is a middle-aged black woman, a tourist from Texas, who's saying over my wife's screams, "Honey, I've got this. You sue him, honey. You sue him good. Lord, I hope the car don't blow up." The video is a little shaky, but my wife's screams are clear—not even screams, plural, but one long wailing sound, like all her breath is draining out of her, all her life in that one howl.

The woman comes a little closer to the wreckage with her camera, and now, finally, my wife is visible. She is still holding onto the wheel, ten and two, her back is straight, not touching the seat, and there is blood dripping from a large gash on her forehead and smearing her left eyelid. She is staring at something I can't see, and her mouth is open so wide, it looks like her jaw is unhinged.

"Oh, Lord. Oh, Lord," the woman filming keeps repeating.

The old man turns to her and says, "I don't know what to do. Should I back up the car? What if it—"

"Explodes? Oh Lord."

"No, no, I mean what if she's hurt, her leg or something, I can't see, I can't see." He paces. Comes back, shouts, "You alright, lady?"

Then the police sirens, the ambulance. An officer comes toward the woman, puts his hand over the camera lens, and asks that she turn it off. She does, but she waits until the Jaws of Life rips the door of Azniv's car; until one of the paramedics carries her like she's a child, her arms around his neck, into the ambulance; until someone tells her my wife's name.

A week after Azniv comes home from the hospital, we get the video in the mail.

For months, my wife will demand to watch the video of her car accident every night. And every night, she'll ask me the same question. She asks, "Do I really sound like this?" The question makes me uncomfortable, like I know she's asking something else, but I don't know what exactly. I have forever to figure it out, but only a few more months to test my responses. "No, honey, you've never cried like this." "Azniv, you were in a terrible accident." "Sweetheart, I'm so happy you're alive." Each time, she'll hum in reply, not looking at me, her eyes glued to the TV. Even though she won't kill herself for another year, I know now that this was the moment I began to lose her.

I just sat there, for months, in the darkness of our living room, watching my wife disappear.

*

There was a bit of the aristocrat in Azniv, in the way she sat down, gathering her skirts in dramatic sweeps before bending, or the way she sliced the tomatoes or cucumbers when she was in the kitchen—slowly, like she was carving meat, piercing the flesh and dragging the knife carefully through the skin so as not to hit bone. She would wash her hands many times a day. When she woke in the middle of the night to get a glass of water, she'd tug the blanket closer around my shoulders. I would stare at her retreating back, at the billowing silk robe clinging to her waist and trailing after her thighs. She had big hips. She never wore pants. She never sang along to the radio, only hummed. When she heard the violin, she danced with her eyes closed or she wept without sound. She braided her hair with her legs crossed, watching herself in the mirror. She polished her heels with my ancient tools before stepping into them. She kissed my temple. She held the sides of my face. She loved our children's feet. When she came to their beds at night, they raised them for her in anticipation. She encircled their ankles with her long fingers and brought them to her face. She kissed each toe.

*

I did not go to cafés, but I had the day I met her. A coworker at the shoe factory had just found out that his wife had given birth to a healthy boy, and like any man of the time, 1988 Soviet Armenia, his reaction was to invite his friends to a local café to celebrate the news instead of seeing to his woman and child. While the group toasted to his good fortune with vodka, I was sneaking glances at the woman playing the violin in between bites of chocolate torte. I didn't drink as a young man for a very simple reason: I couldn't afford to. I couldn't afford the cake either, but my sweet tooth could convince me otherwise.

I noticed her arms first. Lean, long, bare except for a loose silver bracelet on her right hand that I watched float up to her elbow, fall to her wrist. When I try to explain my attraction to her at that moment, when I try to understand it myself, I can only arrive at stupid answers. I must've noticed how strong her arms were, for example. I was a laborer, after all, who found meaning in Communism and product. I valued order and discipline, polished boots, didn't I? I did. I don't know if I found Azniv's movements graceful or her form beautiful. But watching her play, I must've seen something, felt something more transcendent than what I can prescribe for myself now, something beyond words or reason.

The facts are this: I stood up. I moved toward her. She watched me come. She put down her violin.

*

The final night of 1991. Everyone had come to ring in the new year and wish us goodbye. In two weeks, Azniv and I and our firstborn would leave for America. My parents, who had lived with us, would stay in Armenia simply because they could not imagine leaving. It was a particularly cold evening, but everyone was drunk on schnapps that my brother had brought with him from Leningrad. On the kitchen counter, the leftovers from our dinner were covered with aluminum foil because there was no room in the fridge, it was so full of schnapps and apricots.

Near the school where our boy would go for just four months before we won the lottery, the right to America, there was a lone apricot tree. An hour before midnight, alcohol coursing through her veins, Azniv had stuffed plastic bags into her coat and raced out into the cold. We stood in the doorway, laughing and crying as she skipped down the road, waving her hands all the way, almost dancing. Everything she did, in retrospect, had a musical quality to it. But was it calculated, mathematically determined, the way her hands and hips and mouth moved, or instinctive, inevitable like dark magic? I yelled at her to run faster, that the Winter Grandpa—our Soviet version of Santa Claus—was hot on her tail. Holding tightly onto my leg, our boy, too, cheered her on in the dark.

Ten minutes later, she reappeared, coming through the haze of the light snow that had fallen all day, with heavy bags in each hand, bundled up in her winter clothes, and I imagine the entire neighborhood's children gasped in glee, gazing through their windows, candles flickering, thinking her something fantastical. Our boy certainly did. I still do.

*

Now that she's dead, I go through her life with a highlighter in hand, and I look for reasons. I imagine them. I search for them in all the tapes. I think, here is a sign. Here is something from which

I can make meaning. Here is something I can use to explain to our children. Here is something that I will never tell them. Here is something I won't do myself.

The trouble is, there was nothing particularly alarming about my wife's life. And she would agree.

And perhaps that is why she did it. Nothing special at all.

*

I remember her nails most of all. The long, thin fingers, and those nails, how they curved naturally, evenly, toward her palm, without any necessary rough filing, the smell of it, that low simmering smell of bone and death haunting other women's hands and everything they touched, but not hers. Not yet. She'd paint her half-moons painstakingly white, sitting at our dining table, a colorful advertisement for local grocery stores underneath, dotted squares announcing two-for-one deals that she was too dignified to take advantage of. She'd use tape over the pink parts of her nails, taping her individual fingers to the cheap ad, her palm pressed flat, that helpless starfish. With the slowest, most careful of strokes, she'd fill in those half-moons with polish she'd buy from the Asian makeup boutique down our street, her two indulgences, Frou-Frou-French White and Frou-Frou-French Shine. She didn't blow to quicken the drying. Her back rigid, face turned away, she'd look somewhere, anywhere, but down. She had a perfect nose. I remember this too, taking in the profile of her face and dreaming of a girl. Her nose, I would think. She should have her nose. She does.

Finally, after what seemed like hours to me sneaking glances from the living room, or sitting there beside her, book splayed on the table, she'd take the tape off with her free hand, revealing the nice bow of starch white. In two or three more strokes, she'd add the final transparent polish, never once coloring outside of the pink lines and marring her porcelain skin. We'd wait again for an insurmountable time, then she'd give her hand to me, present it like a gift, and I'd hold her wrist and examine it, turn it palm up, palm down, marvel. But I never kissed each finger at each part it bends, never came near her nails. She'd wrench her fingers away from me if I got too close, worried I would ruin her delicate work.

So maybe this was it. We didn't want to be the one to love the other more. We'd punish each other for neglected demonstrations. When we remembered to kiss, to embrace, to touch, to really mean it when we said *I love you* before going to bed, the other one remembered, too, all the times we didn't.

The polishes cost five dollars each, and she'd go through two sets in any given month, the routine that chipped away the home-made French tip never changing with the seasons: wash and clean and wipe and mop and bathe and bake. Before me, she played the violin. Before me, she worked as a store-girl manning her father's fruit market. Before me, she went to University, but then returned to her father's market because that's what you did.

I like to imagine her now, one hand cupping her elbow as she leans against the counter, the other hand framing her cheek. Her eyes are undecorated, though in the pictures I have of her at that age, they always are outlined with a thin arc of kohl, and extend still, so that neighbors and strangers called her the local Arab, the town cigani, their coy little Cleopatra. But in my mind, she is considerate of her father's workplace, decides against the kohl every morning but Sunday, though she hates the way her eyes look without it, so plain, so dull, so unextraordinary. I imagine her with a single thick braid, tied with yellow ribbon, resting against her chest when she straightens to stretch her back; otherwise it dangles, brushing across her left arm with every exaggerated breath, with every tap of a polished fingernail, as she waits for someone to enter through the door and change her life.

*

I was a shoemaker. One of the nine suitcases I brought with us from Armenia was filled entirely with my tools. She walked into my hammer, lying flat on the carpet, our first night in Los Angeles. And though it did not leave a mark, sometimes I noticed her toes clench involuntarily, like a delayed reaction, an instinct formed too late.

My dream was to open a shoe repair shop in East Hollywood. I dreamed about young actresses with favorite heels, fancy businessmen who wanted their soles rubbed down or raised. I wanted to fix shoes, not make new ones. I wanted to correct what another had done wrong or had failed to preserve. But who needed shoes fixed in Los Angeles?

In Armenia, I had wielded hammers for a living.

My skin was deceptive. It made me look like I spent years toiling under the sun in fields, ripping things from their roots, a Tolstoyan son. She liked the look of me, she had said, liked what it could suggest. But what did it suggest exactly? What could it suggest that I couldn't live up to? If only she had said.

In Los Angeles, this meant I looked Mexican, but only to those who were blind to the blue of my eyes. I shaved the stubble from my face every morning, razor up, then razor down, razor up, then razor down, not stopping to rinse away the cloudlet of shaving cream building on the blade. I tucked my shirt in, even at home, even under sweatpants. I grew up sleeping on the stone floor with my three brothers because the eldest had heard it would make our backs strong.

In Los Angeles, I worked for an Armenian jeweler in Downtown that paid me three dollars an hour, and I was grateful. No, it was this. This, precisely. I took everything that was given to me. I swallowed it down. Was this her revenge? Did she think as she stuffed her mouth with all those pills, sweet husband, let's see you accept this?

I worked weekends, too, but what does it matter? We all have stories like this.

When I came home from work, I'd lie on the floor for more than an hour, waiting for the pain to subside. She would join me, and yet that's when we felt the most apart: my eyes closed, her eyes open.

Just what was she looking at? Just what had she seen?

*

When our first child was born in Armenia, the nurses fawned over his chubby cheeks, protruding from underneath his white bonnet. My parents and her parents congratulated each other while my wife slept. Next day, at home, my mother showed my wife how to swaddle him, and Azniv's mother bit her tongue. For forty days, my wife did not leave the apartment. Our boy was a crier, and for a year my wife did not sleep. For a year, I moved my pillow into the living room.

I am sorry, Azniv. Can you hear that? It didn't matter that I had to wake at dawn.

I was paid for how many shoes I made. Every time I branded my identification number on the sole of the shoe and put it down, I was a copek closer to giving her the life she dreamed of. They sat me in the corner of the room, the only one surrounded by walls on both sides, so that I could shame the ninety-nine other shoemakers. Platforms in the summer, fur boots in the winter, piling beside me, my only companions. I was a confident man. I took home my work. I spent the evenings after dinner pounding leather into place. Before, she was impressed.

You don't tire of it, she would say with awe. Or maybe it was not with awe at all.

My wife hushed and hummed and she rocked and she patted. She put our boy beside her in bed, hoping he'd roll into her softness and find comfort there. She pushed down on the mattress hard, and he'd shift, a little, but she couldn't keep pressing down forever.

He always finds his way away from me, she says over breakfast.

How can the night be so quiet when he's screaming, she asks. The room feels bigger. I look into his scowling mouth and want to scream into it, she says. I want to frighten him into silence.

And I nod, chewing, wiping the hammer on my lap with my sleeve.

*

One night, she made a hammock from a beach towel.

A muted cream color, the towel had broad strokes of brown and deep olive green roses in its center. It was made in China, and back then, that was really something. Her dowry was collected since birth. Nightgowns, handkerchiefs, linens and duvets, tablerunners and towels. Towels for every occasion.

Our boy was crying, just crying. He did not want her nipple. My wife smeared honey on her breast and put it in the boy's mouth. From the living room, I watched him lick and lick, spit when the sticky substance was all gone, cry when he tasted her on his lips.

Our home in Armenia had one bedroom and an enclosed balcony. I enclosed it myself, screeded the cement, put brick upon brick, painted it a light blue to open it up, make the room as big as the sky. I was engaged to be married. I was going to bring a bride into the home. I did not expect her to sleep on the floor with me despite the good it would do our backs. My brothers were gone, one married to a Russian woman in Leningrad, the others gone for good. It was up to me to look after my parents. The youngest son. They deserved the bedroom and they didn't argue.

So I worked to build a new bedroom for me and my bride. I put brick upon brick. I painted blue over gray. Brick upon brick. Blue over gray.

I watched my wife, like all women, gaze into her closet looking for an answer. She saw the Chinese beach towel rolled into a ball behind the yellowed bedsheets neatly folded into a square, the ones we first had sex on. My mother had waited outside of our door, and hearing the end, she walked inside, asked us to stand, and pulled the sheets from under us. Outside, she inspected it for blood in the light of the bathroom lamp.

Was my wife embarrassed? I don't care for the traditions of old women, I told her. I love you, I had promised. You are my wife. And she stood there naked, covering herself with her hands, and I could only think how beautiful she looked, how beautiful as she looked into my eyes, as she covered herself, how beautiful in our makeshift bedroom, how beautiful under our makeshift sky.

My wife put our boy in the center of the beach towel, pinched the four edges in her fists. Slowly, like she was dusting or dancing or showing off a trophy, she swung him back and forth. She saw the length of his body in the large gaping triangle. She followed the triangle with her eye, bending her head to look down at him. She swung and she swung. She didn't smile. She kept swinging. She looked up to see me watching. She didn't smile. She kept swinging.

*

In the living room, I find more tapes. The TV is in the middle of an entertainment set, a large glass panel on both sides, each panel split into four levels, each level full of cassettes. My first big purchase in America: a video camera. I wanted to capture everything. I catalogued. I numbered. I described. I bought stickers. Gregori in front of the encyclopedia, 1995. Suzy's baptism, 1993. Palm trees for our trips to the beach. Dice for Las Vegas. The kids made fun of me.

Azniv didn't understand. You're never here, she'd say. You're always behind that thing.

What do I matter, I'd respond happily.

I pick a tape at random. I want the surprise. Maybe then a kind of revelation. I won't have time to brace myself.

The VCR swallows the cassette, and the screen goes blue. I'm on my knees on the carpet.

The screen changes. The colors multiply on my forehead, swirl and shift. And there you are.

We are seated at our dining room table, the four of us. It is Suzy's fifth birthday. You will not see her sixth. The square table sits four. For Suzy's sixth birthday, the square table sits three. Suzy's next to you, Gregori next to me. The tripod is secured a few feet away, in the living room, facing us directly. On the table, a fresh bouquet of carnations, white and pink, in a small clear vase—I bought it for our daughter. Tomatoes and cucumbers make a smile on a plate, a dollop of hummus for the eyes, with paprika sprinkled densely inside for the pupils. We're having pizza, Suzy insisted, but you insisted on some vegetables, too. We are using our fancy wine glasses, though there is no wine. A bottle of Coca-Cola peeks from behind the vase.

You're smiling, talking directly to the camera, looking straight at me from the screen, turning every so often to smile at our daughter, turning away from me.

A toast.

Grow healthy, grow beautiful, grow strong, my daughter.

Suzy smiles at you and raises her glass, accidentally knocking it into the vegetable plate. She turns to me, blushing, and I lean forward to rub her head, my chest pressed against the table, and my tie dips and slides in the hummus. Suzy giggles. I blush, too, and then I laugh. Gregori eats his pizza and pays us no mind.

You look into the camera, and I know, I just know it, you are happy.

I press pause.

*

The first man to fall in love with my wife was just a boy.

He had a kind face, she told me one day out of the blue.

Not even a hint of mustache, she said. Big, round, black eyes, the longest of lashes. When he'd close his eyes, they'd touch his cheek.

The summer before he is drafted into the Soviet Army, he tells her he loves her, and she laughs. It is a hot afternoon; her braids stick to her back. She laughs. He tells her how much heat the body can stand. She apologizes.

Can I, he asks, touching her face.

She nods. She lets herself close her eyes, embraces what will come, thinking it a kindness, to both of them, a goodbye.

This is my wife's first kiss.

He went to the Army and returned tough, she said. Taller somehow, too, with more hair on his face. Gone were those lashes, but his eyes had kept their shadow, his eyes had darkened.

He knocked on my door the evening he returned, Azniv's mother explains. He gave me a letter. It was a poem for her.

Was this the same poem my wife would recite at parties, drunk, for years, years before her accident? Barely able to stand, swaying in place, she never once forgot the words.

I didn't read it, Azniv's mother says.

She never smiled when she was drunk.

It was something about snow falling, her mother says, Wasn't it?

Snowflakes, I tell her. She never forgot the words.

She chose you, her mother says.

She says this time and time again. She says this to me now. I call her on nights like this when the blue glare of the television and the red of the Corvette that pins my wife inside her car, that forces her hands to remain on the wheel, her mouth open in an animal howl, when all these colors, the orange of the apricots weighing down the plastic bags, the bright white polish of the tips of her nails, the silver bracelet sliding up her arm, the brown of the violin once on her shoulder, the muted hues of the beach towel, Suzy's pink and white carnations, the dark of her first lover's eyes, the blue of our fake, fake world, when all these things amount to absolutely nothing at all.

Yes, but why me, I plead with her mother.

I don't know, she answers. Why her?

*

I don't want to forget anything, Azniv. The scar above your eyebrow, your perfect nose, the splatter of freckles around your belly button. How quickly you'd burst into goosebumps when I kissed the back of your neck. Your nose whistling in deep sleep. Your toes curling. Our children's toes curl now, too, Azniv. They wait for you at night in their beds.

What can I tell them? You left them the knowledge of your death but not of your life. You left the door to the bedroom open. Why, Azniv? They still had their backpacks around their shoulders. An accident, I hope. I hope that's all this was. Because now I can't even direct them to the tapes. I can't say, Azniv eating barbeque, 4th of July, '94. I can't say, Azniv diving into the pool in her purple one-piece, the one with the attached skirt, '95. I can't say, Azniv slow-dancing with her son, '92. I can't say, Azniv meeting her daughter for the first time, '93.

I can't say, Azniv ever laughing at a joke. I can't say, Azniv ever meaning it.

You waited for someone to enter through that door and change your life. Well, it's done now. You did it. All gone.

TRANSCULTURATION, OR: AN ADDRESS TO MY AMERICAN LOVER

Love, you want to know everything about me. You want to dig out the pomegranate seeds that line the length of my skin and taste them bursting in your mouth. You want to breathe in and out between my parted thighs and fill your nose with my foreign air. I see you studying the maps. You like to tell me about my people. Darling, I appreciate your enthusiasm. The way you devour the meat of alligators and growl when you kiss me. How, in the mornings, you dream of waters rising and make love to me as if you are drowning, your legs kicking madly until your head falls back, gasping in relief.

Remember, love, that night in Spain? We had just met. On the back of a bar napkin, you asked to see your name, and I showed you. I showed you everything. Oh, but why do you keep it? It hangs now above your bed, thumbtacked to the wall, next to your grandfather's flag, but you are not your grandfather. Your flag is red and white, and it is blue. But I'm colorblind, you say, laughing, and I want to smack you hard. I want to hear the sound of your jaw breaking.

Sweetheart, you want so much of me, but I've got nothing left to give. And you're not mad, I know—just disappointed. I'm not what you expected at all.

The problem, dear, is this: all you know are stories. All you want are fairytales, happy endings. Tell me your stories, you say. I want to hear your stories.

I can give you facts, lover, instead. I can give you definitions, lists, history lessons for boys who love us sad Armenian girls. Pieces you can take, rearrange, and put up on your wall, create a picture to remember me by, point out to your friends that this is the woman I loved and this is why she left me. I'm putting them on paper because I don't trust myself anymore, not my voice.

Darling, I have never treated you like a child, so why won't you stop picturing me as one? I was never a little girl, running down desolate streets, trading bullets and bruises with the neighborhood boys. Or maybe I was, but that's not who I am now. Or maybe that is, but that is not who I wanted to be. That is not who I wanted to be with you.

Lover, are you still listening? I know this is only in English, but I need you to pay attention.

SPITAK EARTHQUAKE, DECEMBER 7, 1988

The Russians call us suicidal, but we are just a people accustomed to loss, that one-winged bird. It has pattered our chests with thin little feet. It has lived with us in cages with open doors. It has filled our bodies with the most desperate of songs. We are a people who eulogize for bread, but we are not martyrs. You're still confusing me for others. We don't die for God, for anyone but ourselves. It is a talent we have, a skill. We do it without warning and without consequence.

You see, on that cold Soviet winter night, we thought we were under attack. We think we are always under attack.

The first wave hit the town's sugar processing plant, and it imploded in a cloud of tiny particles and sharp debris. Those of us on the streets ran towards our collapsing homes. Those of us in our homes sought refuge in our crumbling stone churches. Those of us in our churches then died on the stairs of hospital buildings, going up.

The Azerbaijanis, we cried. The Turks!

Now imagine the air, cold and sweet. Our little boys and our little girls in their school uniforms, opening their mouths, eager to taste candy, finding concrete. Imagine the ancient scabs below our feet opening, widening, pulsating and swallowing. Imagine the roads transforming into mountains, valleys, into rivers. You want fairytales, lover. Imagine the Euphrates rising. Blood sticking to bones. The smell. Imagine the smell. Arms, thumbs, graceful necks buried under blankets of snow, no priests to bless their souls, no children to pour earth over their coffins. There was no more earth. No bright sun either. The sun did not come out for days. And when she reappeared, so too did my people from beneath these blankets. Imagine having to say goodbye again, over and over again, for days, for centuries. Imagine the world collapsing on top of you, the world splitting in two beneath you, a sister calling out a sister's name, a sister not even looking back. Imagine not knowing which way to turn. Imagine not knowing where to run. Imagine not knowing how to live.

THE DUDUK

The duduk is the voice of my people. I know, dear one, how much you love it when I say "my people." How you can hear it perfectly in your head. It's all so very sweet.

The duduk is a double reed instrument with ancient origins, almost three thousand years old. It is made from aged apricot wood that grows alongside the river Arax. This is the instrument with that low, low drone, that sound which gives you pause, the instrument which makes your hair stand on end when you watch those movies you love about gladiators and Gods.

The duduk, dear one, captures the grief of an entire civilization. Did you know we used to make it out of the bones of our mothers? For when the duduk is singing, she is crying, she is lamenting. She is mourning her sons who have been lost to wars. She is mourning her daughters who have been lost to strangers. She is mourning her mountains who have been lost to neighbors. If you close your eyes and you sharpen your ears, you can hear her.

Say it, lover. I know you want to say it. Taste the word between your teeth. Mouth it slowly.

Duduk.

Duduk.

Duduk.

Is that your heart beating? Is that mine?

LIST OF FAMOUS ARMENIANS

• Charles Aznavour, the French Frank Sinatra, born Shahnour Vaghenag Aznavourian. Named Entertainer of the Century in 1998 by CNN, beating out Elvis Presley and Bob Dylan.

• Andre Agassi, famous tennis player, Wimbledon champion. His father is part Armenian and Andre is Armenian enough.

• Principal Seymore Skinner, character from *The Simpsons*. Lover, as a child, I looked into the television screen, into the face of this yellow-skinned man, felt my heart swell with pride.

• Jack Kevorkian, professional euthanizer. America's favorite mercy-killer.

• Most of the men from System of a Down, a hard-rock band based in Los Angeles. The lead singer is famous for his distinct and piercing scream. Extraordinary, a *Rolling Stone* journalist once described it. How can one man vocalize so much pain?

• Cher, diva extraordinaire. Though she's half and she almost lost that half when she got the first of her many nose-jobs. But there's something about Cher, isn't there, darling? Still so distinctly Armenian?

TITLES OF FAMOUS CHER SONGS

Believe. Dead Ringer For Love. Do You Hear What I Hear? Half-Breed. Gypsies, Tramps & Thieves. How Long Has This Been Going On? A House Is Not a Home. If I Could Turn Back Time. Will You Love Me Tomorrow? Hard Enough Getting Over You. A Different Kind of Love. Let This Be A Lesson To You. Strong Enough. Heart of Stone. We All Sleep Alone. Song For The Lonely. Does Anybody Really Fall In Love Anymore?

MY MOTHER'S FINAL WORDS BEFORE THE CANCER TOOK HER BREASTS, AND THEN, HER BODY

Daughter, do not knock on the doors of deceitful men. Wipe away all traces of sand from your hair and give your gravedigging teeth some rest. Stretch out endlessly. Daughter, let your eyes grow blind. Daughter, deafen your ears.

Love, you know this about me, that I was twelve when I moved here. You know this, you are reminded of this, every time I speak. I am too. You love my accent and you say so often. What you may not know is the list of things my parents allowed me to remember of my life back in the village. Our neighbor Stepan, for one, the way he swung his cane through our raspberry bushes on his way home and never apologized. Or my dog, Jolie, who would eat these raspberries and then throw up all over our Persian carpets because we couldn't bear to let him run around outside like the animal he was. Or the fact that at the beginning of every month, a man with a powerful mustache would come to our door, find a flaw in our house's construction and open his hand to negotiation.

Love, there is nothing romantic about the life I lived before I lived here. Please stop asking me all these questions.

A LINE FROM OUR MOST FAMOUS POET, PARUYR SEVAK, FROM ONE OF HIS MOST FAMOUS POEMS, *MENK KICH ENK BAYC MEZ HAY EN ASUM*

I've transliterated it for you, darling, so you can hear the sounds, so you can repeat them. You never did learn how to read or write in my language, though you bought all those books and cassettes. And my mother, bless her heart, she never said, "I told you so."

Parzapes mahn er mez siraharvel

Simply with us, it is death who has fallen in love

Now, don't you go and do something foolish like tattoo this on your arm, try to explain to me how beautiful you think it really is, how you did it for me, all for me. I know well enough the curves of those ancient letters. I recognize what the empty spaces between these words really mean. That there is nothing more to my people than tragedy. That this is what you see every time you look at me. That this is what is written clearly on my forehead. Don't you dare go giving me another reminder, lover. I have enough.

AN EXERCISE IN TRANSLATION

No one says "I love you" in Armenia. Please do not argue. Do not tell me the phrase you learned from books, *Yes sirum em kez,* when we are having sex. The authors got it wrong. They forget—we are a serious people. Sit forward, lover. Grab a pen. This is important. This is what we say, instead:

Hokid mernem. I would die to save your soul. *Tsaved thanem.* Let me please bear your pain.

Matagh linem kez. I would surrender my body to God. I would let the priests sacrifice me. I would let them fill my pockets with stone and force me to wade in. Let my throat be slit and body be boiled in salted water. I would let the earth take me into her mouth, swallow me whole.

The thing is, dear, when you say you love me, I don't quite understand what you mean. But when you say *Yes sirum em kez,* I hate you more than anything.

MONICA

Lover, I loved a woman long before I loved you.

Monica was a short woman, and inside our house, in our bed and in my arms, she was even shorter. There, she didn't wear the three-inch heels required from her at work, where she spent six out of her eight hours thinking about her blistered feet, wincing as she took orders and pocketed tips. Sometimes I would tell her to put those pumps back on. *"Loca gringa,"* she'd say. "You like seeing me in pain, *no?* I don't play that game."

What Monica did play was Good Catholic Girl while I watched. Kneeling in our kitchen, in front of a small statue of la Virgen de Guadalupe, she would cross herself three times with pinched fingers. The flickering light from the candles Monica had placed near the statue's feet made the red blush on its porcelain skin look more like a bruise. Every time I blinked, it changed color—a deep purple, a dark blue, a nauseating green—so I did my best not to. Instead, I tried to focus on the statue's eyes. The Virgin, however, never met my gaze, never even tried. She was content to merely look down onto her tiny ceramic hands clasped in acceptance. Why this is how the world chose to remember the mother of God, at the moment of her resignation, I never quite understood.

One night I awoke in a sweat to find Monica staring at me. I offered her my breasts, and she took them to her mouth, her tongue writing elegant prayers against my peaks. Monica claimed my body was a holy land. "I declare it," she said, pressing a finger against my sternum, her beautiful, black curls, the hair I so loved, falling over my skin. "I worship it."

"That famous mountain of yours—what is it called again?" Monica asked casually. Ararat, I reminded her, suddenly uncomfortable. I rubbed one hand against my damp breasts. The air in the room was colder now, much colder. "Ararat," she repeated. "Funny, isn't it?" she said calmly, poking at my left breast. And I nodded, hating her, slapping her finger, knowing what she was about to say.

ARMENIA AS THE BIRTHPLACE OF CHRISTIANITY

It goes something like this: God decides to flood the Earth after seeing how corrupt it has become. He tells a righteous man named Noah to build an ark and fill it with his family and two of every animal known to him. The world floods. The ark and its inhabitants survive and, after the waters recede, come to rest on a mountain. This mountain is Ararat, the highest point in the Caucuses. The family disembarks and thus begins a new, Christian civilization.

You know what happens afterward, lover. You've seen the maps. I don't need to tell you. You probably know more than I.

THINGS I KNOW EVEN LESS ABOUT, IF ANYTHING AT ALL

The names of my people's ancient kings

My great-grandmother's hair color. Some say we were blonde, before the Turks, though I know this is not true. The beards of our men have always been black. But still, I wonder. Maybe. You can never be too sure of these things

What it means when someone tells you that you're interesting

What men in bars are thinking when they ask to touch my knee

Whether I prefer sleeping or being awake

The rate the world is spinning around me, spinning and spinning. Is this why I feel so dizzy, lover? Is this why I feel sick to my stomach when there is no real reason?

If Monica ever loved me

If you really love me

If I really love you

DIASPORA IS A DIRTY WORD

I think it's why I have such trouble pronouncing it, dear. Why I stumble over those crashing consonants. Why I never know where to place the emphasis, a cute little accent. It never comes out right. You think my struggle's charming, pinching my cheeks. Ironic, even. I think it is a sign from God.

Is there a difference between leaving a place and leaving a person if you leave them twice?

FALL OF COMMUNISM. PART 1

In 1991, the Russians leave our land and we are left on our own for the first time in centuries.

FALL OF COMMUNISM. PART 2

It is our turn to leave.

FALL OF COMMUNISM. PART 3

This time, it was a choice.

THE GENOCIDE

WHAT MONICA SAID THAT NIGHT THAT MADE ME LEAVE HER

"How can you call a mountain yours when it doesn't even reside in your own borders?"

SURVIVOR'S GUILT

Noun. A strong feeling of guilt often experienced by those who have survived some catastrophe that took the lives of others; derives partly from a feeling that they didn't do enough to save those who died and partly from feelings of being unworthy to have been chosen to live.

Lover, why do you always look at me like that? With your sad and beautiful eyes? As if I am the only one in the world for you? I am not that clever. My jokes are rehearsed and my wit researched. Darling, my body is not what it once was. My breasts sag, my thighs tremble and my hands are rough from work. I am not that pretty. My face is plain, lips small, eyes brown and dull and typical.

Do you remember our first morning together in Spain? I'm in my bathrobe, standing in front of the mirror, tube of liner in my hand when you step behind me and say, "I love that you do your eyes like this." You kiss my shoulder, then my neck, my mouth, nose. You pause before my eyes and I find myself closing them. You blow on them gently, drying the black kohl against my lids, your breath warm from sleep. But when you move even closer, touching your lips to my eyes, I feel the ink on them melt away.

I don't remember what happens afterward. If you brush my smeared eyeliner away with a hard thumb, or if you shape the darkness with your tongue, so that there is still a flick in the corner, still a hint of what I looked like before you walked on over.

QUESTION I GOT WRONG ON MY INTRO TO WORLD
GEOGRAPHY FINAL

What are the straits connecting the Mediterranean Sea to the Black Sea?

The correct answer: The Bosphorus (also called the Istanbul Strait) and the Dardanelles.

I wrote, instead, who gives a shit? O to be young and arrogant, to be ignorant and happy. Some of us learn things we wish we didn't know, dear. Some of us want to teach others these very lessons. Some of us are lonely in our despair. Some of us want company. Or maybe this is not it at all.

THE QUESTION MY PROFESSOR
SHOULD'VE ASKED ME

Where was your great-grandfather Armen loaded onto a barge and then sunk?

Or, an alternative, a few years later: Where have you been kissed so deeply as to feel nothing at all, not the tips of your fingers, the sun coloring your back, the fists buried deep in your hair, all that water crashing around you, all of that water, bloody, all that time, but you, you didn't even notice.

THE NAGORNO-KARABAKH CONFLICT

Azerbaijan and Armenia are two women who kind of resemble each other and want the same man. Their breasts are plentiful, their hair is dark, eyes, darker. Azerbaijan, however, is the sister of the Armenia's ex-lover, Turkey. The women had gotten to know each other when Armenia and Turkey were dating. They had gone out for coffee, danced like dervishes in each other's bedrooms, spinning wildly with their arms spread apart, their fingers tapping rhythmically against the other's after every turn. They had done each other's nails. But when the man and woman broke up—a terrible split, devastating, really—Azerbaijan felt the rumble of blood boiling inside of her, reminding her her choice was made: family first. So the women grew old and they grew apart, and then, years later, they fell in love with the same man.

This man, his name is Karabakh, doesn't really know who he wants, what he wants, because, well, because he's just a man. The women foolishly try to poison one another, forgetting the sounds their fingers made years ago when they would connect, when they would find each other in the air, the little sparks of recognition they made when they made contact. Both women end up dying. It's all very Shakespearean, lover. The man, in turn, contemplates death for decades because he feels like now no one will ever want him—for who wants to love an eyewitness to murder, a mere, lonely bystander? Funny thing is, the ghosts of these women still do. They're still fighting over him, pulling at each other's hair with long and transparent arms. You know what's funnier? The man wasn't all that special to begin with.

Here's what is not funny: how many of us died for no good reason, for a land that wasn't even fertile, for a black garden. How many men left our warm bodies in order to seize the ground that would breed no crops or children. And when they left, the men left us hungry and wanting. They forced us to drain our own bodies dry.

We placed our hands between our thighs and pushed.

We placed our hands between our mouths and sucked.

We placed our hands over our breasts and pulled.

When they returned, lover, they returned to ghosts.

Diaspora is a dirty word. The dirtiest. Especially when it's a choice. The wrong one.

AFTERMATH OF THE QUAKE

When I look at the small scar above my eyebrow, lover, the one you gently trail with your index finger, I like to pretend the wound is from the heater in our old living room that I ran into after skidding across the wooden floor in my new, smooth-soled slippers—a 10th-birthday present, maybe, from my father. I like to pretend it's not from the chandelier hanging over our dining table, a rococo beast with eight hands that held just as many bulbs. I like to pretend it's not from when it crashed onto the ground next to me, two of its hands breaking from their tissue and rushing towards my face. I like to pretend that when I heard my younger sister's scream, I stopped, looked around, tried to search for her, tried to pull her body from under the rubble. I like to pretend that I did not just leave her, that I did not just leave her there, at seven, gray and dusty and broken. I like to pretend my parents were glad to still have found one, to still have found one of their two alive. I like to pretend Monica's black, curly hair was unique, exotic only to her. I like to pretend I never brushed hair like hers before, maybe sitting on an ancient, ugly couch, a little girl with eyes like mine, a nose like our father's and a big, toothy smile, sitting between my knees, leaning her head back into my lap.

There are stories we tell ourselves to lessen the guilt. There are stories we dream up so may never have to get out of bed and face the mourning. And there are stories, too, lover, that we create for one another, tales we weave because we don't believe in the real thing. We were never allowed to.

My hand is dark, dear, and yours is not—be glad. My history is my own. You see, when we hold hands, when you dig your fingers into my palms, I worry you are trying to dig my past back up. I worry that you want to claim some of my land for yourself. Not to discover a place for us to live on, a common ground, a lover's nation, but because you're searching for treasure.

But I am no man's gold. I am no man's bursting oil pipe. I am no prize. I will not make you rich. I will not make you worldly, the envy of your poor and ignorant friends. I will not be a picture on your wall. I will not be a name next to a flag. I will not be another place you've simply been, a body you've crossed and conquered, a country you can call your own.

You will not mine me.